That Birthday in Barbados

That Birthday in Barbados

Inglath Cooper

Contents

Copyright

Published by Fence Free Entertainment, LLC

Cooper, Inglath
That Birthday in Barbados / Inglath Cooper
ISBN – 978-0-578-50595-4

This is a work of fiction. Names, characters, places, events, locales, and incidents are either the products of the author's imagination or used in a fictitious manner. Any resemblance to actual persons, living or dead, or actual events is purely coincidental.

Fence Free Entertainment, LLC
Fence.free.entertainment.llc@gmail.com

Publisher's Note

This is a work of fiction. Names, characters, places, and incidents are a product of the author's imagination. Locales and public names are sometimes used for atmospheric purposes. Any resemblance to actual people, living or dead, or to businesses, companies, events, institutions, or locales is completely coincidental.

Books by Inglath Cooper

That Birthday in Barbados
That Month in Tuscany
Swerve
The Heart That Breaks
My Italian Lover
Fences – Book Three – Smith Mountain Lake Series
Dragonfly Summer – Book Two – Smith Mountain Lake Series
Blue Wide Sky – Book One – Smith Mountain Lake Series
And Then You Loved Me
Down a Country Road
Good Guys Love Dogs
Truths and Roses
Nashville – Part Ten – Not Without You
Nashville – Book Nine – You, Me and a Palm Tree
Nashville – Book Eight – R U Serious
Nashville – Book Seven – Commit
Nashville – Book Six – Sweet Tea and Me

Nashville – Book Five – Amazed
Nashville – Book Four – Pleasure in the Rain
Nashville – Book Three – What We Feel
Nashville – Book Two – Hammer and a Song
Nashville – Book One – Ready to Reach
A Gift of Grace
RITA® Award Winner John Riley's Girl
A Woman With Secrets
Unfinished Business
A Woman Like Annie
The Lost Daughter of Pigeon Hollow
A Year and a Day

That Birthday in Barbados . . .

What is it about turning forty that makes a woman take a look at where she's been and where she's going?

For ActivGirl CEO Catherine Camilleri, it is a crossroads that has her wondering where she went off course. Divorced without children, life isn't what she had pictured for herself twenty years ago. Not up to admitting any of this in front of friends and family, she bails on the surprise party being thrown for her and books a last-minute trip to Barbados for a stay at the luxurious hotel where she'd spent her honeymoon ten years before. Is she going back to mourn the marriage she'd thought would last forever? Or in an attempt to chase out of her heart for good a betrayal that forever changed her?

Anders Walker might be just the ticket for that. After a brief career on Wall Street and a life experience that turned his world upside down, Anders took off the golden handcuffs and walked away for good. When he spots Catherine checking in on arrival at the hotel, he challenges her to try his spin class. He sees a woman who no longer considers herself someone a guy like him would be attracted to. Except that she's wrong. In Catherine, he recognizes a woman who defines herself by rejection. He sees, too, that she has made work her life. But he's learned that there is so much more to living. Simple things like swimming with sea turtles. And watching the sun sink on a Caribbean horizon. He's got two weeks to prove it to her, to make sure she will always remember that birthday in Barbados.

Map of Barbados

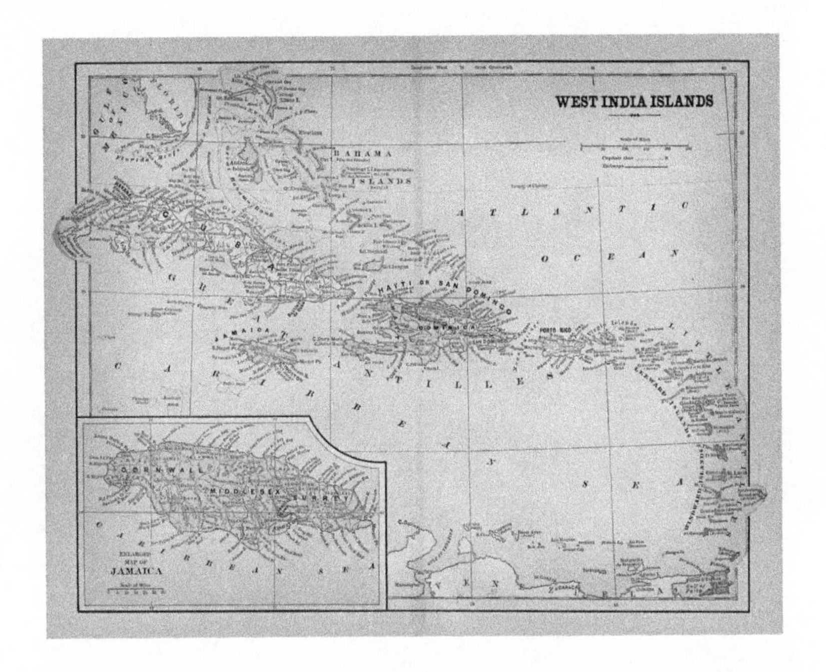

Prologue

"My life is a train and it has derailed."
— Amelia Mysko

Catherine

LATER, I WOULD ask myself how betrayal could go completely undetected, unless, of course, I was simply naive or considered myself someone that kind of thing never happened to. And I guess, in all truth, it was both.

But that morning, on the day my life changed forever, I never imagined it happening to me.

That morning, I was thinking about other things. It was a big day. A huge day. A day I'd dreamed about but never believed could actually happen.

I would have loved to sneak into my office, close the door and give myself a private pep talk. But as soon as I stepped off the elevator, everyone knew I'd arrived `a la the click-clack of the Louboutins I rarely took out of the closet. I usually showed up in workout clothes, but on this day I had to look the part of CEO. And they were all staring at me because they knew today was different. In the hours ahead, I would be completely changing our company culture from small, private company to publicly held cog in a much larger wheel.

At the tap of my heels, heads bobbed up, smiles broke out, hands got busy tapping keyboards. Someone yelled out, "We're going public, baby!"

The words sent a missile of apprehension cruising through my stomach. I smiled and gunned it down the hallway, click-clacking the entire way. Outside my office, my assistant, James, vaulted from his desk and grabbed the cup of Starbucks he'd picked up for me from the store near our building.

"You look ravishing this morning," he said, following me. "Those attorneys you're meeting with rate better than yoga pants?"

"First impressions," I said, taking a sip of my still hot coffee. "And I can handle one day on Wall Street without my running shoes."

The glass door to my office was wide open, and I stepped inside, shivering. "Why is it always freezing in here?" I asked, setting my coffee on the desk.

"You're freezing. I'm sweating," James said, wiping the back of his hand across his forehead.

"It's New York. I'm not sure I've been warm since the day I moved here."

"It's that South Carolina DNA," he said. "And you need more body fat. That's your main problem."

"And your problem is that you stay out late partying. You're detoxing before my very eyes."

He barked a laugh. "You should try it sometime. All work and no play— "

"Keep Catherine from having a hangover," I asserted.

"And from having a good time," he added.

"With the current work load here, I'm afraid a good time is not in the cards for me."

"Have you ever thought about slowing down? Like hitting the brakes and taking notice of the trees outside your window? Well, actually, the trees in Central Park."

I leaned back and gave him a look. "Are you trying to tell me something, James?"

"You know what they say. There's more to life than work. Take babies, for example. Don't most marriages get to a point where a baby is the next step?"

"When would I have time for a child, James?"

James shrugged, looked out the window where Manhattan skyscrapers glared back at us. "Yeah. I know. It's just that I've been listening to a book by Dr. Wayne Dyer on the train coming to work. Dr. Dyer said, "Anything you must have, owns you. When you release it, you get more of it."

"More work?" I teased.

"More life, I guess."

"Do you think that's true?" I asked, serious because he's serious.

"Maybe," he said.

I tapped the keyboard of my Mac desktop and brought up my calendar screen. "Do you think this business owns me?"

"Some days," he said without hesitating. "Most, actually, if I'm truthful."

At the sober note in his voice, I looked up from the calendar. "ActivGirl is my baby right now. I've created the little monster and slowing down isn't an option. I'm getting ready to sign the next five years of my life away."

"Yeah. I've been thinking a lot about choices lately. How every single one we make links to the next choice. And together all those choices make what ends up being our lives."

I gave him a questioning stare. "What exactly did you have to drink last night, James?"

He smiled a half-smile, shaking his head. "Deep for me, huh?"

"A bit for your age. But why do I have the feeling there's something more than an audiobook behind this sudden insight of yours?"

He chewed on his lower lip, looking worried and then trying to clear his expression. "I'm sure it's nothing."

"What's nothing?" I asked, a funny flutter hitting the center of my stomach, my inner radar sending up a sudden sonar blast.

"If I say something, and it's nothing, I'll feel like a real jerk."

I considered shrugging this off. Something told me I should. That I'd regret not doing so. But I wasn't made like that. Once the red cape appeared in front of me, I couldn't ignore it. "Okay, 'fess up," I said, trying to keep my voice light. "What is it?"

He looked down at his hands, rubbed his palms

together, and then pressed them against the sides of his head. "Oh, crap. I wish I hadn't said anything."

"James. Whatever it is, just say it."

I saw the struggle on his face, the deep desire that he wished he'd remained silent. The equal realization that he was already in the curve, and it was too late to turn back now. Nothing to do but accelerate.

He exhaled. "So I stopped off at the Plaza Hotel yesterday after work to meet a friend for a drink."

"Yes?" My heart pounded. I could feel it beating against the wall of my chest, hammering my temples. I was standing on the tracks, and I could hear the train coming, see it too, but I couldn't move.

"I really don't want to tell you this," he said, and it was clear he wished he'd stayed quiet.

"James. Please." Even as I demanded that he say whatever had him so undone, I wanted him to stop. I wanted to pause the moment. Rewind to ten minutes earlier when I walked out of the elevator, thinking the only possible kink in my day could come from a deal falling through.

James bit his lip, visibly struggling, and then leapt off the ledge. "Connor and Nicole were having drinks at one of the back tables."

"What?"

And then relief flooded through me, liquid, golden. I laughed, hearing my gratitude for the reprise. "Oh. I bet they're planning something for my birthday. Those two— "

"Were kissing. Passionately."

The words fell on me like boulders from the sky. I felt the blood leave my face. I tried to form the word *What*, but my lips wouldn't move. I stared at him, images crashing through my head, the cut line of Connor's jaw, my sister's pretty mouth, his hands on her face.

"Catherine?" James said my name on a note of panic. "Here, sit down." He put a hand on each of my shoulders, guided me to the chair at my desk. "Don't faint! Please don't faint!"

I leaned my head against the back of the chair and drew in a deep breath. I prayed that I didn't humiliate myself by passing out. I tried for a word, couldn't find one, shook my head. "Are you . . . are you sure?" I finally managed.

James stood above me, looking at the puddle I'd dissolved into, as if he had never regretted anything more than this moment. "Dear God, I so wish I weren't, Catherine."

I nodded once, hard, pressed my lips together and said, "Okay, then. On with the day. Would you mind going to the fourth floor and picking up the rest of the documents I'll need for the meeting?"

"Yes. Yes, of course. It's just that you're getting ready to make such a big life change, and I thought you deserved to know in case. . ."

"It's okay, James. You were right to tell me."

Looking now as if he were going to cry, he left the office. Alone, I caught my reflection in the silver-framed mirror hanging behind my desk.

Suddenly, I saw the circles under my green eyes. And were those wrinkle lines at the corners? When did they appear? Did I need Botox? I'd hated the very idea, but maybe I'd been an idiot.

I've lost my looks.

There. The truth.

My shoulder-length blonde hair was in need of a cut, and could use some highlights. My skin was at its most pale winter hue.

When was the last time Connor and I made love?

The question struck me from nowhere. A lightning bolt illuminating truths I had been ignoring for months now like dirty laundry tossed to the back of the closet. If I didn't acknowledge the problem, it wasn't a problem.

Connor didn't want me.

I thought he was tired. Overworked. We needed a vacation. A getaway. A reconnect.

But that hadn't been it at all. He'd been having an affair. With my sister.

The shock of this truth hit me like a hammer in the heart, betrayal the nail being pounded into its center. My husband. My sister.

A scream formed at the base of my throat, but I swallowed it back, afraid it would tear the walls of this office apart.

Instead, I reached for my laptop, popped open the lid, entered the pass code at the main screen. I tapped the search engine icon and entered Connor's email account service. At the login page, I entered his email address, my fingers hovering over the password box. I knew it at one time. But he changed it a few months ago when he received a notice saying someone had tried to login to his account. Or had that been a lie?

I tried a combination of his social security number

and our wedding date. It took a few attempts. I hit the jackpot with the last string. I marveled for a moment how well you could know a person when you'd been together as long as I'd been with Connor. And, too, how you could not know them at all.

Once I was in, I glanced at the new emails. Mostly junk. There was one from Ed, Connor's college roommate. I started to open it, decided not to.

I clicked on Old Mail, scrolled down the list, stopping at the sight of my sister's email address.

My thumb hovered over the keyboard, the silence in my office now blaring in my ears like the roar of a jet engine.

I could leave it.

Would it be better not to know? Wait until the meeting was over today and then talk to Connor tonight? Maybe there was an explanation. Maybe James misread the situation.

But then it would be difficult to misread a passionate kiss.

Before I could change my mind, I clicked on the email and opened it. A chain of communication between my sister and my husband unfolded before my eyes.

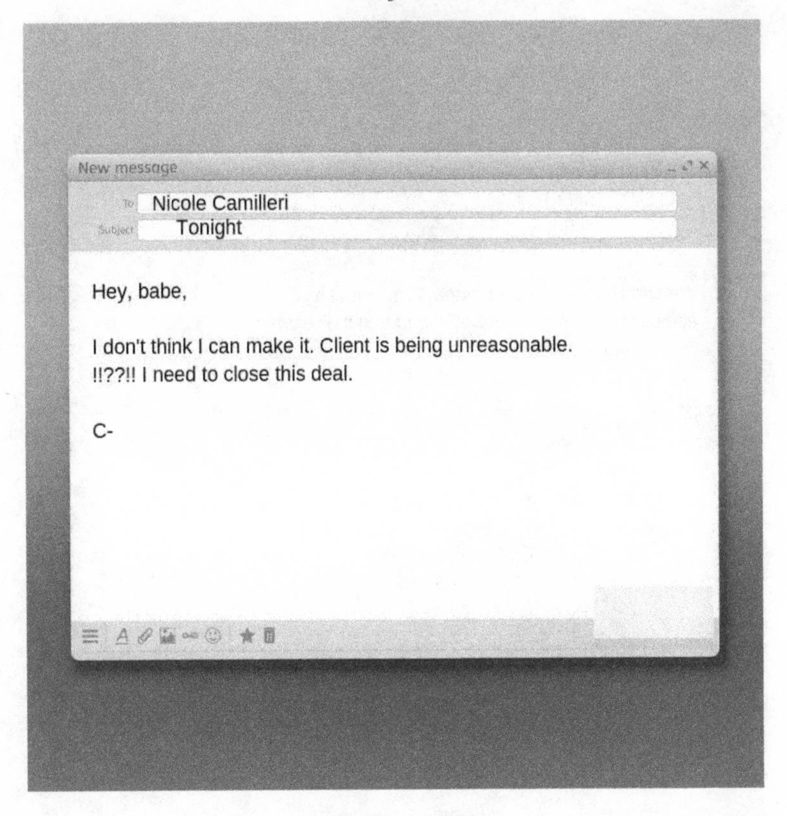

I sat for a moment, staring at the words, trying to absorb them. Slowly, I backed out and clicked on the next one.

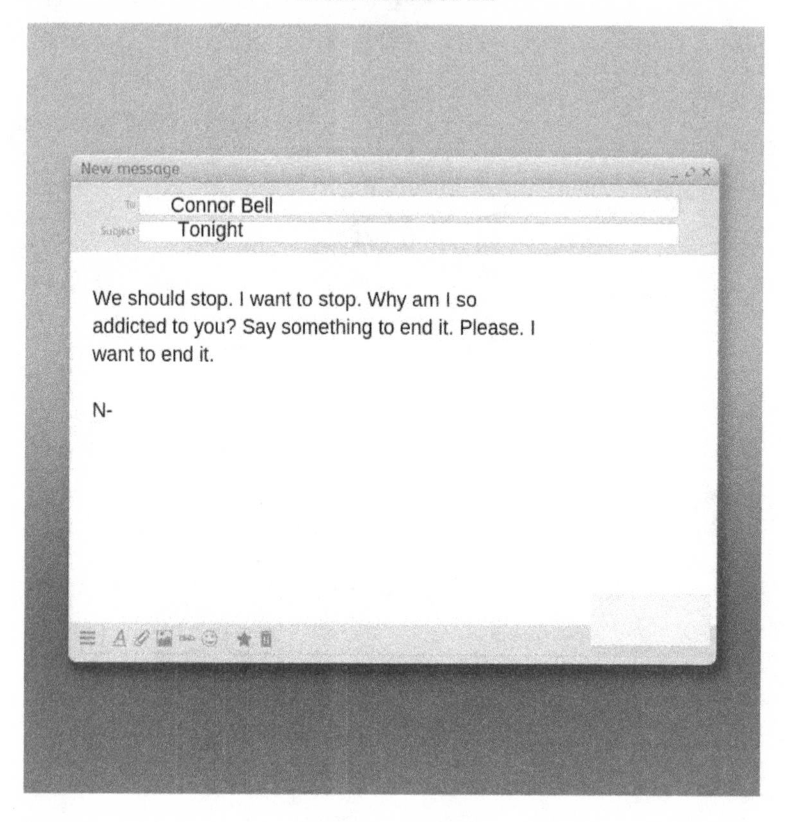

I'd opened a Pandora's box, but I didn't have the power to close it.

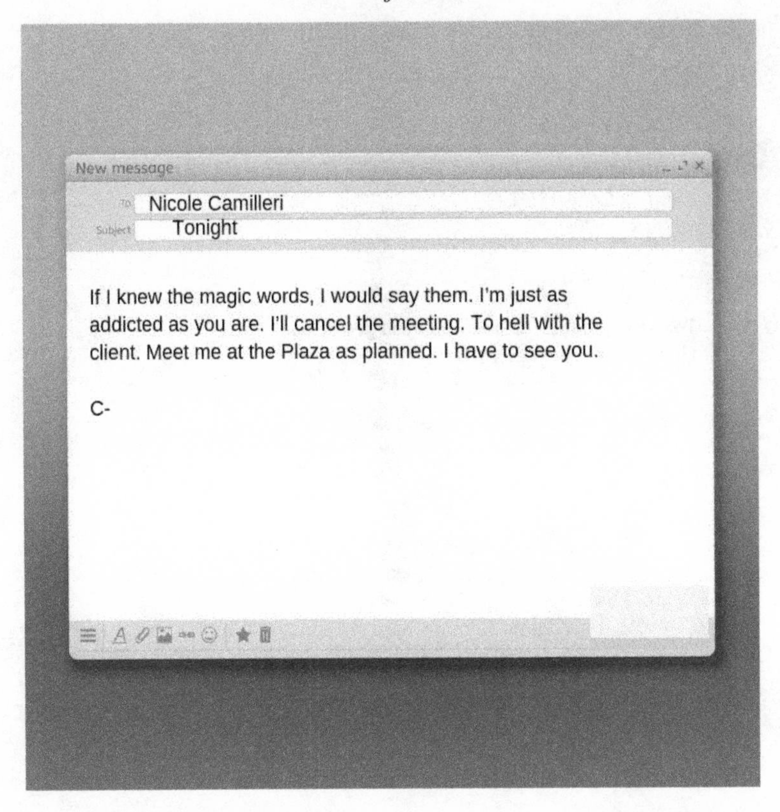

With my hand shaking, I forced myself to open the next one.

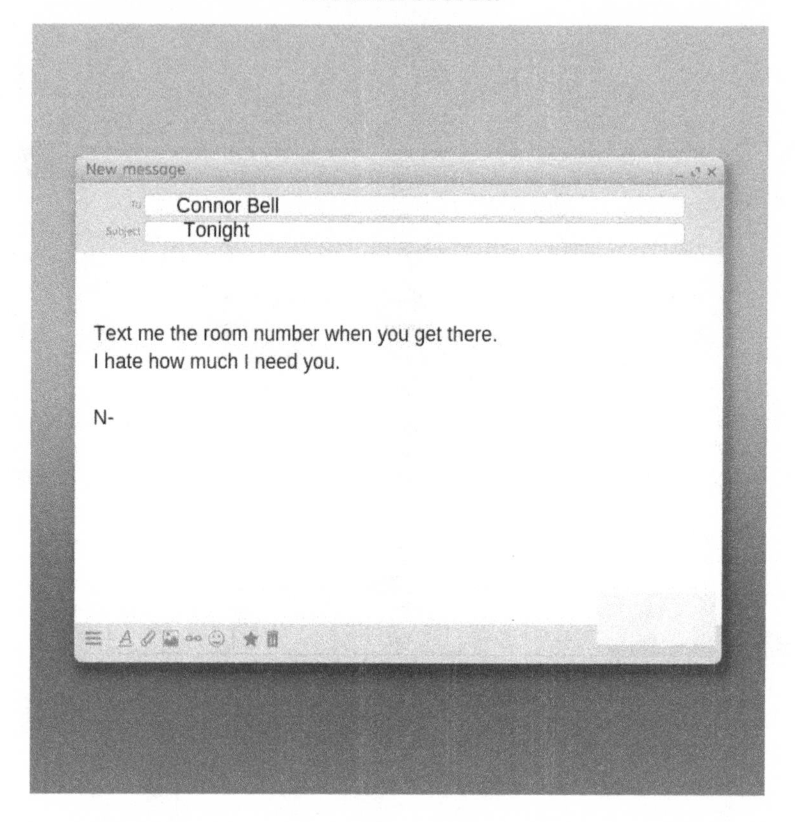

I stopped there, closed out the account. I couldn't read anymore. My stomach rolled.

I bolted from my chair. I barely made it to the toilet in the office bathroom before throwing up the coffee that was the only thing on my stomach.

I retched so hard that it felt as if a knife was cutting through my midsection.

When there was nothing left to come up, I stood, pushing my hair back from my face. A knife might actually have been less painful than the reality of betrayal.

My sister. My husband.

I pictured both their faces, heard their voices telling me the lies that had been necessary to keep all of this secret. How long had it been going on? When did it start?

Another stab of pain hit me in the center of my chest. I bent over, wrapping my arms around myself, squeezing as hard as I could, as if my very soul were dissolving and flowing right out onto the floor.

Suddenly, I had no idea who I was, the threads of my life unraveling until the fabric was no longer recognizable. My knees buckled. I lay face down on the floor, arms outstretched, Louboutins slipping from my feet. They were now nothing more than proof that I had spent the past fifteen years of my life building a company that had taken all of my energy and focus. So much so that I had been blind to the fact that the two most important people in my life had gone on without me, forged something new and separate from me.

And that left me . . . alone.

I raised my head and allowed myself a slow take of the corner office signifying the pinnacle of my life's work to date. And all of this for nothing.

A sob rose up from deep inside me. I coughed it out as if my body were trying to reject some foreign bacteria it recognized as deadly.

I started to cry, the tears streaming down my face with such force I was all but certain they would never stop.

Chapter One

"My soul can find no staircase to Heaven unless it be through Earth's loveliness."
– Michelangelo

Catherine

Three years later

THEY DO STOP. Eventually, I ran out of tears.

I mull this fact, staring out the window of the first-class seat, studying the clouds below with an objectivity I never before had about flying. I used to feel real fear for getting on a plane, would dope myself up with Benadryl as soon as I took my seat so I could sleep through as much of the flight as possible.

But I don't feel fear anymore. And I don't cry anymore. The tears I'd nearly drowned in the morning I'd come face to face with the end of my marriage are long gone. Once they finally stopped, they never started up again.

Because I don't feel much of anything these days.

I've read plenty of books on grief in the past three years, and I've learned that people who experience tremendous loss sometimes turn off their ability to feel. I've wondered, more than once, if I've turned to stone. Like one of those poor souls who stared at Medusa and got zapped into rock, never to feel a single thing again.

Maybe it's for the best, anyway. It's better not to feel. Feelings don't stay static. What starts out as happiness, given it hangs around long enough, inevitably evolves into sadness. And if anyone knows that the first one isn't worth the second one, it would be me.

"Have you been to Barbados before?"

The question startles me out of my cloud staring, and I turn to glance at the woman sitting next to me. She's dressed in an off-white pantsuit with a vivid orange blouse showing at the edges of the lapels, a perfect match to her lipstick. Her makeup is perfect too, and she's smiling as if happiness is her middle name. "Yes," I say. "You?"

"Oh, yes. It's my favorite place anywhere in the world. I go as often as I can. Where are you staying, dear?"

"The Sandy Lane," I answer.

"Spectacular. You've stayed there before?"

"Once," I say.

"I've spent three honeymoons there. Each with a different husband. Outlived them all, I'm afraid."

"Oh," I say, instantly regretting my inner grouch. "I'm really sorry."

The woman shrugs. "One of those inevitable facts

of life, I'm afraid. I'm just grateful to have what I had with each of them."

"You're going alone this time?"

"I am," the woman says. "Better alone than not at all. Are you meeting someone there?"

I shake my head. "No. Birthday present from me to me."

"Nothing wrong with that." She sticks out her hand. "Madeline Evers."

I extend my hand. "Catherine. Camilleri. Nice to meet you."

"You're awfully young to be celebrating your birthday alone. When you get to be my age, you expect it. But you–"

"I'm actually happy to be alone."

"Oh." Madeline studies me for a string of seconds, as if she doesn't know what to make of what I've just said. "You're very sad, aren't you, dear?" she finally says in a soft voice.

I blink once, reach for the paperback I'd stuffed in the seat pocket in front of me, open the cover, keeping my gaze down. "Isn't everyone in one way or another?" I reply on a half laugh.

She reaches across to cover my hand with hers. "No, dear. Not as a way of life. Sure, this journey has its ups and downs. But happiness comes back. If we let it."

Sarcasm dances on the end of my tongue, but she's too nice for me to indulge the temptation. I look up and smile at her instead, and she chuckles.

"I can see you don't believe me. But if I've learned

anything from the losses in my life, it is that I get to decide when I'm willing to open a new door."

"But won't the same thing end up being behind that one too?"

She considers this for a moment. "It's undeniable that we're all leaving this world one day. But I don't believe we're meant to be lonely here." She starts to add something else, then shakes her head a little. "He really hurt you, didn't he?"

I could deny it, brush off her insight as false, but what would be the point? "We spent our honeymoon at the Sandy Lane."

"Ah."

"Odd I would come back, isn't it?"

"Not at all, actually."

"You know it really isn't like me to drown a stranger in my cynicism," I say, a little sorry to put a damper on her mood.

"It's okay. Maybe that's exactly what you need to do at this moment, and I'm sitting here because I'm the person you're meant to be sharing it with."

I glance at her again, wish I had it in me to exhibit the type of kindness she is showing me. "You believe in fate?"

"I believe that we meet certain people in our lives when we're meant to."

I think of Connor and our first meeting and wonder what the purpose of that had been, other than the eventual destruction of my life.

"I can see what you're thinking," Madeline says, wagging a finger in the air. "If I'm right, then why do we meet the people who bring us great pain?"

I don't deny it, letting my gaze voice my touché.

"Because we have vital things to learn even from those people," she declares.

"Those are lessons I'd just as soon skip then."

"Wouldn't we all?" she says on a soft laugh. "But when you get to where I am in life, you realize that we are who we end up being because of each and every experience we've had. To pull one would unravel the entire masterpiece."

I laugh a little, thinking of the declaration James had made in my office that morning three years ago. Dr. Dyer had been right. "I don't think I'm going to end up being a masterpiece."

"Ah, but you can be. I try to imagine that the tsunami waves of life are smoothing out my sharp edges, making them round and accepting like beautiful sea glass."

"How old are you, Madeline?"

She answers without hesitation. "Eighty-one."

"Really?" I ask, failing to hide my astonishment.

She laughs. "Every minute of it."

"I would never have guessed that."

"Then I hope it is because I am wearing my life well instead of it wearing me."

I think about those words long after Madeline has settled in her seat and closed her eyes for a nap. I look out at the clouds below the plane and allow myself to remember that I used to be someone very different from who I am today. I wasn't bitter. I was trusting. I wasn't resigned. I was hopeful. I realize too that I do not like myself now. Not even a little bit.

I think of my financial accomplishments, the very

large sum of money sitting in my investment bank account. If I quit working today and lived a life far more extravagant than my current one, I would never spend all of it.

That is what I have to show for my choices. That is who I am.

I glance at Madeline, note the soft, peaceful expression on her remarkably unlined face. I envy her contentment, her acceptance of what has been and what lies ahead. I envy her ability to seek out joy again, even when it is not guaranteed.

I once had something of what Madeline has inside me. I know I did. Along with the other losses I've grieved in the past three years, I feel a deep pang of mourning for the death of the woman I used to be.

Chapter Two

"From the same window, you keep seeing the same view!"

— Mehmet Murat ildan

Catherine

AS IT TURNS out, Madeline and I are both greeted by a pretty young woman in pink as we enter the customs area. Her smile reminds me of the sun, bright and warm. She is holding up a Sandy Lane Hotel sign with our names on it and introduces herself as Elsa.

"Welcome to Barbados," she says with a lovely lilt to her voice. "Let's get you through the paperwork stuff, and then we'll get your luggage and head outside where we have a van waiting to take you to the hotel. No need to waste time here when you're ready to enjoy your vacation."

We both thank her, and she leads us around the throng of passengers to a booth where our passports are screened, and we are quickly checked through.

We wait a few minutes at the luggage carousel while Madeline and Elsa make small talk about the weather in New York and how wonderful it is to escape the December cold.

I think about checking my phone, but find myself unwilling to turn it on because I'll have to answer questions about where I've gone, when I'll be back, and I don't want to. For the first time in longer than I can remember, I'm glad to be disconnected from the city and the life I've left behind.

My suitcase appears on the conveyor, and I step forward to get it, but at Elsa's direction, a young man picks it up and loads it on a cart. Madeline's luggage arrives within a couple of minutes. Elsa leads us through one more checkpoint before we head to the van. As we step outside the airport doors, I remember the freezing air as I'd climbed out of the Uber car early this morning and feel a wash of relief for the humidity and warmth here. I can practically feel my skin sigh with appreciation. Elsa speaks to the driver and wishes us both a wonderful stay at the Sandy Lane.

The driver holds the door for us. We climb in, and he walks around and gets inside, offering us bottles of cold Evian water. "Buckle up if you don't mind," he says, smiling at us in the rearview. "It's required here."

We both snap our belts, and I gratefully sip from my water as we head away from the airport and into Barbados.

I can see the ocean in the distance. The area near the airport is suprisingly rural. Homes are scattered here and there, cows tied in surprising places, grazing small patches of brownish green grass. This part of the island feels like a place where people live instead of vacation. Within a few minutes, we pass a grocery store and a strip mall with store names I don't recognize. A truck parked on the side of the road is loaded with coconuts. A man stands at the tailgate. Using the end of a pickaxe, he slams the coconut against the tip until the hard outer shell cracks. He then passes it to a woman who sticks a straw in the center and takes a sip.

Madeline remarks that little has changed since she was here last, and I have to agree with her. I try to remember what it felt like to make this drive from the airport to the hotel with Connor, but my mind cannot seem to clarify the recollection. Is it gone, or was I still too hung over from our wedding reception for my brain to permanently store those moments? That, or I've just refused to let myself remember a time when I had been so happy, or at least believed I was.

I put my focus back on the road ahead of us, glad when I begin to recognize the landscape near the hotel. The driver hits the blinker, and we are turning into the gate entrance of the Sandy Lane. A guard waves us in, and the familiar building is suddenly there in front of us. My heart kicks against my chest, and I feel both elated to be here and as if I am going to burst into tears. Madeline glances at me, reaches over and squeezes my hand. "I have a feeling this will be a special trip for you, my dear. Just give it a chance, okay?"

I nod once, biting my lower lip. "I hope it's wonderful for you," I say.

"I don't plan to let it be anything other than that," she says, smiling at me.

I half expect to blink and find Madeline gone in a poof, as if she is a figment of my imagination. Her bulletproof optimism seems too perfect to be real, but despite my cynicism, I can't deny being glad to see that it still exists in the world, even if I can't imagine myself ever feeling it again.

The driver stops the van at the main entrance, and two young men in hotel attire step out to open the back and remove our luggage. The driver opens the sliding door and offers a hand to help us out.

Pink is the hotel's signature color, splashed about on chair cushions and table umbrellas, on the accent pillows propped against white chairs. It's not the pink of cotton candy and ballerina slippers, but a deep vibrant fuchsia that brings to mind Florida bougainvillea and the dragon fruit of Central America.

The main entrance offers us a view clear to the Atlantic Ocean. It is breathtaking. I have not forgotten this. I have a sudden yearning to run straight in, swim to the platform bobbing peacefully on the aqua water and lie there face up with the sun blazing down on me. Maybe it would finally chase the coldness from my bones, thaw the frozen stone where my heart used to be.

A beautiful young woman greets us at the entrance, bringing me back to reality. She is dressed in pink and carries a tray with icy glasses of an equally pink, fruity drink. She hands us each one, and waves us to the reception desk where two attendants begin to check our reservations.

Madeline finishes first, and another pretty young lady in a pink dress steps forward to walk her to her room. "I am sure we will see each other," Madeline says, giving me a quick hug. "Enjoy, my dear."

I watch her walk away, feeling a little sorry to see her go. Or maybe it's that I fear all the positive energy she has doused me with will go with her. The attendant continues typing something into her keyboard, assuring me it will only be another minute.

Steps sound on the marble floor behind me. I glance around, my gaze colliding with a pair of beautiful eyes. I hang there for a moment, thinking how similar they are to the sea I felt so tempted to throw myself in. Realizing I'm staring, I drop my own eyes, and then there's a voice.

"Welcome to the Sandy Lane. Spin class tomorrow at eight o'clock. Hope to see you there."

I look at him fully, and wilt a little beneath the smile accompanying the words. "Oh. I don't know. Maybe."

"It's a great way to justify the indulging," he says, his voice low under an American accent.

I try to place the region and come up with a somewhat neutralized New York.

"Which I assume you're planning to take advantage of?" he adds.

"Yes. I imagine I will."

He's standing right in front of me now, sticks out his hand. "Anders Walker."

"Catherine Camilleri."

"Nice to meet you," he says and then tips his head, a question crossing his face. "Wait. Camilleri. You started ActivGirl?"

For a moment, I'm too surprised to answer. "I-yes. How did you-"

"I remember when you filed to go public a few years ago. I used to work on Wall Street."

"Oh."

He hears the question in my voice, smiles, and says, "And now I'm teaching a spin class in Barbados. Yep, there is a story attached. You come to my class tomorrow, and I might tell you sometime."

I smile at his teasing, surprising myself with, "You've piqued my curiosity. How can I not show up now?"

"Right. Because you definitely won't get away with saying you don't have anything to wear."

I laugh a light laugh, the sound strange to my own ears. How long has it been since I laughed unexpectedly? I no longer think of myself as someone who laughs. I think of myself as someone for whom that is a thing of the past. I sober, as if he might pick up on this, find the laughter false. "Ah, okay. I'll try to set my alarm to get up in time."

"And I'll look forward to seeing you there," he says, backing up and then with a wave, heads out the front entrance and jogs toward the spa that sits just across the paved road.

The young lady who greeted us with drinks walks

up and says, "Ms. Camilleri, your room is ready. I'll be happy to walk you there."

"Thank you," I say, picking up my purse and laptop bag and following her across the off-white marble floor.

"You'll notice the wet floor signs," she points out as we head for the hallway leading to the stairs. "We have quick showers that come and go and can make the marble quite slick."

"Thank you," I say.

"You're on the third floor with a wonderful view of the beach," she says.

I follow her up the stairs where she uses a card to open the door. I step inside behind her, relieved to be here. The room is luxurious, a view of the ocean visible through the open curtains that lead to a private porch.

"Your luggage will be here shortly," she says. "Shall I have someone unpack for you?"

"Thank you, but I'm all good, thanks."

"The refrigerator is stocked with drinks. And there's ice in the bucket just there. I hope you have a wonderful stay at the Sandy Lane, Ms. Camilleri. If there's anything we can do for you at any time, just call the front desk."

"Thank you so much," I say.

She leaves the room then, closing the door quietly behind her. I fall back onto the bed, staring at the ceiling as a wave of sudden fatigue hits me. I compare the room to the one Connor and I had on our honeymoon. This one is much nicer. We weren't on the oceanfront then. Extra money had gone back into the business, and we felt fortunate to be at the hotel at all, our honeymoon a definite splurge.

I close my eyes, and a memory comes floating up. A very nice attendant had escorted us to our room then as well. No sooner had he closed the door than Connor said, "Finally."

He unbuttoned his shirt, grabbing the bottom and tearing it off over his head. He'd walked straight for me, pushed me onto the bed and pulled off my clothes, one deliberate piece at a time until I lay naked on the bed. He stood, unzipped his pants and then removed them altogether.

I stared at him, unable to take my eyes off him. It was the first time I had seen him this way. We'd waited until marriage, wanting to save the first time, for it to be as special as our love for each other.

He lay down next to me, running his hand over my shoulder, around the curve of my breast to settle at my waist. He kissed me then, long and slow, and I can still remember how it felt, the way I had wanted to stay there with him forever, loving and being loved.

My eyes snap open now, and I stare at the ceiling above me. Not for the first time, it seems a shame that memories cannot stay with us as they were. That what comes after has the power to reshape what seemed right and true at the time. But betrayal does that. It's the rust that corrodes and collapses and requires us to see that what we thought would last forever never really had a chance of doing so.

Muted laughter floats up now from the beach

below my oceanfront room. Children's laughter, happy, carefree. I wonder what would have happened had Connor and I made a baby on our honeymoon here. Would we still be together? Would our lives have taken a different track? Would I have seen my business differently, not let it become the focus of our marriage?

Tears well up and slide down my face. I don't bother to wipe them away because it's been so long since I cried, I'm almost glad to know I still can.

But what is there to cry about?

I married a man who turned out to be someone I didn't know at all. A man who chose my sister over me. If there's anything to cry about, it's my gullibility. That I'd actually thought love lasted forever.

It doesn't.

If it exists at all, it won't last. And if you don't expect something to last, it can't hurt you when it finally decides to leave. Sorry, Madeline, but that's the real truth.

*

I WAKE TO A knock at the door.

I open my eyes, reluctant to yield to the pull toward consciousness. I pull myself up on one elbow, noticing the darkness now serving as a backdrop to my porch view. What time is it?

I squint at the clock next to the bed. 8:45. Oh gosh.

A voice sounds from the door. "Housekeeping."

I get up, still in my travel clothes and go to open

it. The woman standing on the other side smiles at me. "Turn down service?"

"Ah, yes, please," I say. "Thank you so much."

"Do you need fresh towels?" she asks.

"No. I'm all good on that."

She walks to the sliding glass doors and closes the curtains. When she begins to tidy the bed, I say, "I'm going to take a shower. Thank you so much."

"Have a good evening, Miss," she says with a smile.

I step into the bathroom and close the door, flicking on the light to stare at myself in the mirror. Oy. The nap didn't help.

A marble shower sits in the far corner of the room. I walk over to turn on the water, adjusting the temperature. I shrug out of my clothes, grateful that I won't be wearing heavy winter things for the next two weeks.

Two weeks.

I should have booked a shorter stay. There's no way I won't go stir crazy with that much relaxing. If I can even remember how.

I step into the shower, turn my back to the warm spray and then tip my head to let the water run across my hair and down my face.

Fourteen days of sitting on the beach. I can't quite imagine.

I think about the spin class, that gorgeous man's face popping into my mind.

Had he been flirting with me?

No.

Definitely not.

He was being nice. It is his job to be nice to guests. To get people to come to his class. He probably gets paid based on how full it is.

I recognize my own cynicism and try to remember a time when I wasn't this way. When I could meet a man and not be suspicious of intention. B.C. Before Connor.

I wash my hair with the hotel's lovely-smelling shampoo, rinse it out and add conditioner.

It's been a while since I've done a spin class, but I've always loved them, and I need to work out while I'm here. I'll pick a bike in the back of the room, and odds are he won't even notice I'm there. Even if he does, I'll just be one more guest he recruited for the class.

I get out of the shower, reach for a thick white towel, dry off and then wrap it around myself, searching out a pair of pajamas from my suitcase. My first night at the Sandy Lane and I'm doing PJs and room service. Madeline would not approve.

I'll do better tomorrow.

Chapter Three

"A man is worked upon by what he works on. He may carve out his circumstances, but his circumstances will carve him out as well."
— Frederick Douglass

Anders

I'D BEEN CLIMBING in my vehicle, heading out for the day when my cell rang, and the hotel manager asked if I could pinch hit for a no-show bartender in the upstairs restaurant. At loose ends for the night, I'd agreed, and as I pour gin into an icy glass with one of the Sandy Lane's majestic sunsets bowing out in front of me, I'm hit with a not unfamiliar stab of appreciation for the simplicity of my life.

It's not the one I'd originally set my sights on, but it is the one for which I have no regrets.

I work out for a living, encourage others to do it as well, and when needed, revert to the skill I had relied on to get me through college and an MBA from Columbia.

"What are you making there?"

I glance at the end of the bar to see a man in a white shirt and navy jacket watching me intently. "Barbadian Gin punch," I answer.

"What's in that?"

"Genever, which is like gin, but not. Coconut water, lime juice and bitters."

"Genever?"

"Known as Dutch gin, not to confuse it with London dry gin."

"Ah. Looks good."

"Like to try one?"

"Sure," he says. "The New Yorker in me usually can't get away from the bourbon."

"Nothing wrong with a good bourbon," I say. "But I think you'll like the change of pace."

I finish the one I'm making, set it on a tray for the waitress to pick up and start another. Once I've made it, I walk to the other end of the bar and set it in front of him.

He picks it up, takes a sip and says, "Too bad I had to discover this on my last night."

"Just another reason for you to come back," I say.

He nods. "Wish I didn't have to leave."

"You don't. Have to."

He laughs and says, "I'm sure it looks like that from your point of view, but I live in reality, unfortunately."

"We all do. It's just that our choices create our reality."

"But then you live in paradise. Easy for you to say."

I pick up a towel and wipe off a spot of water from the bar. "By choice."

"Were you born here?"

"Actually, I was born in New York. Went to school in the city. Worked in the city."

Now I have his attention. "Wait. Aren't you the guy teaching spin in the spa?"

"That would be me," I say. "I fill in up here when needed."

"What did you do in the city?"

"Wall Street for a while."

Now he looks as if he doesn't believe me. "Me, too," he says.

"Different life," I say.

"Who did you work for?"

I name the well-known Wall Street firm, note his raised eyebrows.

"That's a fairly big transition," he says.

"It was my dream. I worked really hard to get there, but life had other plans for me."

"So you didn't stay around long enough to get a pair of the golden handcuffs."

"You hold the key, man."

He takes another sip of his drink. "You look awfully young to cash out."

"The sunsets here don't have a price on them."

A look of pure envy crosses his face. But right behind it comes resignation, and I can see that he thinks his own fate is sealed. "It's never too late to make another choice, you know."

"My wife would never understand. She's gotten used to the perks."

"If you work the hours I worked, she's not spending too much time sharing those perks with you."

"No, she's not," he admits. "Nonetheless-"

A waitress appears at the end of the bar, hands me an order. I look at the drink requests and reach for a bottle of rum on the wall behind me. "Hope you get back down soon," I say and then get to work.

I feel his gaze on my back, hear the words he can't bring himself to say. He'd like to walk away. But he won't. And yeah, I feel sorry for him. I've met others like him in the time I've been here. People who've worked hard, accrued enough wealth to come to a place like the Sandy Lane. But they're trapped in their own lives. And if they got a wake-up call, they haven't bothered to heed it.

I think about the woman I met at the front desk earlier, and I somehow know she's one of those people. It's not that hard to recognize the signs and the all but visible imprints of the cuffs. And that what probably started out as a dream for her has somehow turned into a prison.

I should know. I created one of my own. Looking at the guy at the end of the bar, I find myself glad for my wake-up call, despite the hell it sent me to. Without it, I would be that guy. There is no doubt about it.

*

Four years ago

IF ANYONE HAD asked me whether I

considered myself a humble person, I would have said yes. Maybe I would have hesitated before answering. Truly humble people do that, don't they? Appear uncomfortable with any kind of spotlight? Turn the conversation away from themselves?

I don't know if I was uncomfortable with it. I wasn't used to it. Growing up in the foster care system, going to college on scholarship. I got hired straight out of NYU, worked on Wall Street in a firm where I'd had to borrow money to buy the suits I needed to fit in. So yeah, I knew what humility felt like, but after three years of working my way up the ladder and being given the opportunity to skip a rung here and there, I might have bought my own press to some degree.

I was young, on the way to being rich by any standard I'd ever considered a measuring stick, and women seemed to enjoy my company.

On this particular night, a group of us headed downtown for dinner and drinks at Cipriani. We're ordering a second bottle of wine when Ashley Lewis pulls a chair over and wedges it between me and Sam Hawkins, a co-worker who's likely my biggest competition for a next promotion. Ashley tells him to move over, and he does so with a raised eyebrow and a knowing smile directed my way. There's a bit of jealousy etched beneath it.

I stand and help her position the chair closer to the table.

"Hey," she says.

"Hey," I say, sitting back down, and picking up

a bottle of wine, holding it poised over the glass in front of her.

"I'd love some."

I pour her one, stopping halfway since it's fairly clear she's well on her way to being intoxicated.

Ashley started with the firm last year, an MBA out of Stanford, and when it came to the genetic lottery pool, she got more than her fair share of winning tickets. Beautiful enough to be on magazine covers for a living. And smart enough to run her own hedge fund one day.

For the past couple of weeks, she's been letting me know she'd like to take our friendship outside the office. It hasn't seemed like a great idea, but now that she's sitting here next to me, looking great, smelling great, I realize I'm going to have a hard time turning her down.

The place is crowded, and laughter rings out from multiple tables around the room, conversation a hum beneath it. Ashley barely lets me finish answering one question before she tosses me another one, and I recognize her people skills with some admiration. She has no need to turn the focus to herself, and I wonder if this is because she is shy or so confident in who she is that she doesn't need to display insecurity over it.

We share the risotto I'd ordered and are making our way through our mutually agreed up on sides of the plate when my phone pings. I glance at the screen and see a text from an unfamiliar number.

I pick up the phone and tap into messages. I recognize the number as the doctor's office where I had gone for some lab work a few days ago. The blood work had been a non-negotiable part of completing an update to my health insurance policy with the firm. I recall now checking the box that gave them permission to contact me through text and email. The message is short.

Your results are in. Please come by our office between
8 and 10 AM tomorrow for some further testing.

He feels the ping of concern that hits his center. He puts the phone down.

"What's wrong?" Ashley asks. "You look worried."

"Probably nothing. Just getting the results back for our health insurance update."

"What a pain, right?" she asks, taking a sip of her wine. "Everything okay?"

"I'm sure," he says. "Maybe they missed something."

"Yeah," she says, reaching over to cover my hand with hers, as if she senses my uncertainty.

In all honesty, I was grateful for the connection. Before that message, I had no real plans of furthering anything with Ashley. But I went home with her that night. I did not want to be alone.

Chapter Four

"Age is a case of mind over matter. If you don't mind, it don't matter."
— Satchel Paige

Catherine

THE KNOCK AT my door comes at six a.m. Before going to sleep, I'd arranged for coffee delivery as my wake up call, and I trudge to the door, wishing I'd used the clock so I could tell it to go away.

The young man holding my coffee tray looks as if he expects me to be unhappy to see him and enters the room with a cheerful, "Good morning, Ms. Camilleri. You are going to be so happy you woke up for this coffee."

I smile despite my grogginess. "I hope you're right."

"Would you like to have it outside?"

"That sounds wonderful."

He sets the tray down on the desk and opens

the sliding glass doors. He carries it outside then and arranges the service on a marble-top table. "As you can hear, the birds are already declaring it a wonderful day."

"They are cheerful," I admit.

He chuckles while I sign the check, wishes me a good day and leaves me to my coffee. I breathe in the ocean breeze and note the sun rising out of the horizon. I pour myself a cup and stand at the balcony rail to take it all in, suddenly glad I'm up and witness to the day's rebirth.

I remember then it is my birthday. I close my eyes for a moment. Forty.

Good heavens. How did that happen?

I open my eyes again, staring out at the dawning light on the ocean.

It is a breathtaking sight. The hotel surroundings have come alive. Attendants are pulling the chairs from their storage spot and lining them up in the sand, covering each one with the hotel's signature pink towels. They talk as they work, their voices low and harmonic.

Forty, and I'm alone here in the same place where I'd spent my honeymoon, thinking I knew exactly how my life would go.

Could I have been more wrong?

Doubtful.

The coffee is as delicious as predicted, and I pour a second cup, going inside for my laptop and sitting on the small couch by the balcony, reluctant to connect with the world outside this place. But my work habits are too ingrained to continue ignoring email, so I turn it on, find the wireless connection and login.

First in the queue is from my sister. I consider not opening it, as I always do, but curiosity won't let me ignore it this morning. I click in, and there's an e-card with a picture of a big white cake.

Happy birthday, C–. I miss sharing birthdays with you. I hope you'll forgive me one day even though I don't deserve it.

Tears well in my eyes, slide down my cheeks. Suddenly, I miss her so much that it feels like a knife slicing through my heart. I think too about the unfairness of losing not only my husband, but my sister as well.

You could forgive her.

The words dance through my thoughts, not for the first time. Unlike all the other times, they linger this morning because I don't immediately shove them from the realm of possibility.

But how can I?

I can't deny the bitterness rooted in my heart. I feel its presence on a regular basis like bile in the back of my throat. How is it fair it should be up to me to fix something I didn't break?

I slap the laptop closed, severing my connection to the life I've left behind for two weeks. Work can wait.

Work will be there when I get back. It's the only thing that will be, but it's always been enough. A vacation isn't going to change that.

I pull workout clothes from the drawer I'd put them away in last night. I've just finished getting dressed when my cell rings from the nightstand where I'd plugged it in to recharge.

I walk over and look at the screen. It's the Manhattan area code, but I don't recognize the number. I should ignore it, at the least let voice mail pick it up, but I've never been good at ignoring questions, and I tap the answer button with a short, "Hello."

"Catherine. Please don't hang up."

Connor's voice shocks me into silence, and I hold the phone to my ear, waiting.

"I called from a number I knew you wouldn't recognize. Otherwise, you wouldn't have answered."

"What do you want, Connor?" My voice has an edge to it, and I resent him for bringing that out in me.

"Just to wish you happy birthday," he says softly.

"You didn't need to do that."

"I wanted to."

"Thanks. Is that all?"

"Catherine." There's pleading attached to my name, and I'm suddenly irate that he thinks there is anything I can do about his own need for redemption.

"What do you want from me, Connor? Both you and Nicole will have to figure out what to do with your guilt. I can't fix it for you."

"I know that. But wouldn't it be good for all of us if we tried to get to a better place?"

"Where exactly would that be? Sunday dinners at my place? The three of us talking about old times?"

"Catherine-"

"You tore my heart out, Connor. There, I said it. Thanks for the birthday reminder."

And on that, I hang up.

Chapter Five

"Stab the body and it heals, but injure the heart and the wound lasts a lifetime."
— Mineko Iwasaki

Nicole

SHE KNOWS THERE won't be a reply to the birthday email.

In three years, how many messages has she left for Catherine? How many emails has she written, knowing all the while they won't be opened?

Too many to count, actually.

Nicole kicks up her pace along the boardwalk in West Palm Beach. At just after seven, she isn't the only one out early. A woman on a bike pedals past her, going in the opposite direction. She's wearing ear buds and doesn't make eye contact. A dark blue Maserati rolls by on the street, its engine revving a protest against the twenty-five mile per hour speed limit.

It's beautiful here, but for a moment, Nicole misses

Greenville, South Carolina, the town where she'd grown up, with a pang that yawns wide in the pit of her stomach. She could love it here, mainly because of the weather and the fact that blue skies make an appearance nearly every day of the year.

But if she's honest, she's not sure there's anywhere she really belongs anymore. Hoping to give Catherine space three years ago, she'd left New York, moved back to Greenville where she'd been unable to face her own family. She'd reached the point where she could no longer school her expression into sympathetic questioning when her mother had shaken her head and said, "I don't understand what happened with Catherine and Connor. They were such a good fit and seemed to be so in love. And she's too busy to come home anymore. I don't know what to make of it, Nicole."

Whether she'd been standing in her mother's kitchen during a visit, or listening to the pain in her voice from the veil of her cell phone, Nicole's guilt grew with every mention of her sister's divorce.

There were times when she wanted to blurt the entire disastrous nightmare out loud to both her parents, lift the lid to the Pandora's box she herself had created, let them know once and for all what a terrible person their youngest daughter turned out to be.

It would be a relief, really, to bring it all out in the open, to feel the full force of their anger and disappointment.

She deserves it all. And more.

She picks her pace up yet another notch, her lungs

starting to burn from the effort. It feels good though. She likes the discomfort, wishing for a way to keep it on full-time, an external source of pain to extinguish the one inside her that stays at a permanent low burn.

She doesn't think there's anything capable of extinguishing her own self-loathing though. It's something she'll live with for the rest of her life. Sometimes, she wonders what it was inside her that set her on self-destruct? Was it because she herself had never married? Had she been jealous of Catherine?

It's an easy answer. But not a truthful one. Sure, she and Catherine had gone through spurts of typical sibling rivalry. There had been that time when she'd been in seventh grade and Catherine was in the eighth, and they'd liked the same boy. Mark Sanders. He'd been in Nicole's grade, and she'd had a crush on him the entire school year.

He'd ended up liking Catherine, and yeah, that hurt. No one wants to lose out to her big sister. But she had. Catherine and Mark hadn't lasted past Christmas break that year, and by then, Nicole no longer wanted him either.

As for Connor?

That one caught her by complete surprise.

She'd stopped by their apartment in Manhattan one night to drop off a sample for Catherine who had still been at work. Connor answered the door dressed in a T-shirt and shorts and all but dripping sweat from a run on their treadmill. She intended to leave the sample without coming in, but he'd offered to make her a drink, and the thought of returning home to her much smaller, and lonely, apartment was tempting enough to sway her. It was just a drink after all.

But a journey starts with a single step, and that night opened a door to wanting something that was not hers.

She'd discovered they were both lonely.

Connor's hours as an attorney paled compared to the late hours Catherine worked in her own business. Connor didn't complain though. He understood that it was her dream and fully endorsed her going after it.

It was as if before that night, neither of them had ever looked at the other with anything beyond platonic friendship. She wasn't sure they'd really even liked one another.

And yet. . .

She's reached the end of the boardwalk by now. She leans against the railing and stares out at the blue water of the intercoastal waterway. The sun sends a glint of diamonds dancing across its surface.

West Palm Beach is without doubt a beautiful place to live. But for Nicole, it doesn't really matter where she lives. Emptiness fills her, the weight of her own terrible decision-making a concrete block on her chest. She is the prodigal daughter. Only she can't return home, can't repent. Doing so would mean having to tell her parents about her role in Catherine and Connor's divorce.

She would have to admit that Catherine isn't coming home anymore because of her.

Maybe it is time for that. Time to own the consequences of what she had done.

Her stomach lifts, then dips.

Is she ready to see that look of disappointment on her mother's face? Ready to hear that note of pain in her father's voice?

It is selfish, but no, she isn't.

All her life, she's been the one to disappoint their parents. The one who had to write two hundred sentences in detention after school for talking back to the teacher. The one who failed out of college and took a pity job from her sister with her then fledgling business.

Face it, she tells herself. Failure is the only word that applies. She iis thirty-eight years old, soon to be thirty-nine, working as a waitress, no man in her life, no children.

Maybe it is wrong to even try to get Catherine to forgive her. Maybe she is nothing but a rock around her sister's neck, always trying to pull her down to her level.

Is it true?

Had she spent her life afraid to even try to compete with Catherine? Had it been easier to ride on her coattails, take what wasn't hers?

The questions stab at her heart with a knife point of something undeniable.

She pushes away from the railing, running back the way she had come. She picks up her pace, her feet pounding the concrete until her breathing is harsh in her chest. One thing she knows. She will never run fast enough to leave behind the reality of who she has become.

Chapter Six

"It's easier to bleed than sweat, Mr. Motes."
— Flannery O'Connor

Anders

SHE SNAGS MY attention as soon as she walks in the room.

But then it would be hard not to notice her.

The travel clothes from yesterday are gone, and in their place, black shorts, fitted and high cut. The tank top is a light blue, cut low above a black sports bra. She looks uncertain, as if she suspects she's out of her element. Something in that strikes in me a desire to put her at ease, and so I walk over, welcome her with a smile.

"Glad you decided to come. You could've slept in, first day of vacation and all."

She's surprised to find me standing right in front of her, her smile wavering as she glances around the room at the other people chatting and adjusting their seat height. "Ah, thanks. I hope I haven't forgotten how to do this. It's been a while."

"It'll come right back," I say. "We have two bikes left. One up front and one on the back row."

"Back row, please," she says.

"I can still see you," I tease. "Don't be thinking I won't notice you slacking off."

She laughs, surprising me as much as herself, I think. "I'm a bit out of shape. And wondering if I should be in here at all."

"Absolutely," I say, waving a hand at the full class. "When you're done, you can go enjoy that English buffet with a clear conscience."

She smiles at me, her gaze direct now, as if she's trying to decide just how much credibility to give me. It hits me that I care what she thinks. "So," I say. "Let's get your seat adjusted to the right height. Towels in the corner, and bottled water in the fridge. Help yourself."

We head for the bike in the back corner. "Stand next to the seat," I say. "You want your hip to line up with the top."

She does as I ask, and I bring the seat up two levels. "Long legs," I say.

She glances up at me, then drops her gaze, and I swear there's color in her cheeks. Am I flirting with her? She's wondering. Am I? I don't know. Maybe. I like that I've made her blush.

"I think I'll grab a water," she says and heads for the refrigerator.

I walk up front and ask if anyone else needs help with their bike.

"I do, Anders."

I follow the voice to the second row where Gracie

Mathers is looking at me with a big smile on her face. She's a resident of one of the resort properties and a regular in my class. At seventy-three, she likes to play the helpless card, indulging in a little harmless flirting which I can't deny is flattering. She stands next to her bike, and I make the necessary adjustments.

In a voice meant to carry, she says, "You could be an advertisement for your own line of workout clothing, Anders, dear. What man wouldn't want muscles like yours? And what woman–"

"There you go, Gracie," I interrupt her, laughing. "You're all set. And we better get started, or you're going to miss that buffet."

The entire class is laughing now. I tap the iPad screen next to my bike and turn up the music. I climb on, clip in to the pedals and clap my hands once. "Good morning, everyone. I'm Anders Walker, reformed New Yorker transplant, living one day at a time here in paradise. Approximately 5300 miles from the North Pole, 7100 miles from the South Pole and a scant 900 miles from the Equator. Are you ready to bring it this morning?"

Cheers follow the question. I crank the music louder, glance at the back to see Catherine Camilleri already pumping to the beat. Competitive. I would have guessed as much.

"All right, people. You've got a couple of numbers on your screen that matter in our efforts here. The first is resistance. Ideally, you'll be in the range of the number I'm asking you for. Cadence is how fast you're pedaling. I'll be giving you a number to hit, but remember to listen to your own body. Everybody good with that?"

Another roar of approval goes up, and I top it with, "Let's leave some sweat on the floor, people!"

For the next forty-five minutes, I prod, cajole and sweet-talk up the effort level in the room. My goal is the same as always, get the class to give as much as they've got so that when they're done, they feel like they got what they came for and can't wait to do it again.

By the time we reach the cool-down, there's not a single person who isn't sweating proof I've accomplished my goal. The music slows, and I guide them through a series of stretches, finally climbing off the bikes and finishing out with toe touches.

As the last song winds down, everyone claps and I thank them for coming. A few people wipe off their bikes and head out the door, while others linger and chat.

Catherine Camilleri is gathering up her things to leave, but somehow, I'm not ready to let her go yet. I walk over and say in a low voice, "You're lucky I didn't out you."

Her face is flushed from the effort, sweat beading on the skin above the neckline of her shirt. She raises a brow. "How's that?"

"If I'd let everyone know you own a fitness clothing company, you would have owed them a little more effort."

Owned," she corrects. "And are you saying I didn't make enough effort?"

"To the contrary. Proof is in the sweat."

She smiles a half-smile and shrugs. "Turning forty is motivation enough."

"You? Forty?"

"Today as a matter of fact."

"You don't look a day over–"

"Thirty-nine and a half?"

We both laugh then, and I say, "I was going for considerably under that."

"Well, thanks," she says, "but it is what it is, you know."

"Are you celebrating with family today?"

I keep my tone light, as if I'm not fishing for info on who she's vacationing with, but I can see by the way she drops her gaze that I'm not that slick.

"No," she says. "I'm flying solo for this one."

"I have it on good authority that it isn't healthy to spend birthdays alone."

"Ah. Makes you age quicker?"

"Exactly."

Everyone else has left the room by now, and I'm suddenly aware of this in a way that makes me take a step back. There's a current of something between us I recognize as physical attraction. But then I work for the hotel, and she is a guest. I put the necessary line back in place between us, and say, "Well, I hope the rest of your day is everything a birthday should be."

"Thanks," she says, reaching down to pick up the bag she'd brought to class with her. "And thank you for the workout. It was much needed. And really great."

"You did your label proud," I say. "Come back tomorrow."

"If I'm not too sore to walk," she says, turning then and heading for the door.

I watch her leave, something inside me wanting to call her back. But what would be the point? The two of us live in different worlds. Mine is here, for however long I'm around to live it. And hers is in New York City, a place where I can no longer live the life I need to lead.

*

Four years ago

I SIT IN the chair at the far corner of the crowded room. I'm one of twenty or so people laying claim for the day to an off-white lounger backed up to one of the room's only two windows. If I turn my head, I can see the very large Bradford pear loaded with white blooms at the corner of the building. The petals remind me that it's spring. Which reminds me that this is the time of year when I would be running in Central Park. Getting in shape for a marathon. Or riding my bike for a 50-miler.

Thinking of myself as the person who had done those things seems as if I must be dreaming. That person isn't me. Did I ever do that?

I turn my head away from the window and catch a glimpse of the mirror hanging on the wall across from my chair. I see the skeleton of a man reflected there. His face is thin, and it has a grayish tint. He has no eyebrows and no eyelashes.

With a jolt, I realize that man is me.

Next to me in the mirror is a silver stand from

which hangs a plastic bag. It drips its slow poison through a skinny plastic tube that connects to a needle that connects to a tortured vein in my right arm. I watch the bag empty its contents drop by drop by drop, aware that I am being filled with a chemical weaponry smart enough to kill the dividing cells in my body. Apparently, cancer cells divide more often than normal cells, the theory being that chemotherapy is much more likely to kill them.

Some part of me knows that the reason I look the way I do is because normal cells are dying too.

After all, I do look like I'm dying. Which, in reality, I guess I am.

I wonder if the medicine – I loathe using that term for it – is winning the battle or losing it. My guess is losing. Who could declare the way I feel a win?

I've been at this for six weeks, and with every passing day, I know the life is seeping from me. Something outside the window catches my eye. I look. It's a bike in the parking lot. A cyclist in a helmet and skinny pants and a racing shirt. He aims a key at a nearby car, locks it and climbs on the bike. He pedals off, as if he doesn't have a care in the world, and I am hit with such envy it feels like acid eating a hole in the center of my heart.

What is it they say about health? You don't appreciate it until you don't have it. It couldn't be any more true.

Even after I'd been told I have leukemia, the words wouldn't sink in. I didn't feel sick. Maybe I had been a little more tired than usual, but I worked all the time. Everyone in my office was tired.

The doctor recommended I come in the following day to map out a treatment plan. I couldn't imagine what that would be. Pills? Shots? It never occurred to me that I would become a patient who spent his days in a room with other patients just like him. That I would lose my hair, my eyebrows, my eyelashes. That I would drop forty pounds and that people would fail to recognize me in places I frequented and was known, like the grocery store and a bookstore on my street.

It was as if once I was told I was sick, I was.

In the chair closest to me, I hear a woman sigh, a long, pain-filled sigh that ties my heart in a knot. I don't want to look at her, but I do, and tears spring to my eyes, blurring my vision. I blink them away and ask her if she is all right. She lets her gaze meet mine, and I see in her eyes what she already knows. She will not survive this. If I look like I'm losing the battle, she looks as if the other side has already won.

Our gazes lock, and there is nothing but truth between us. I let her see I know what she knows. I want to cry for her, but she does not want me to. All around us are other patients in various stages of fight and defeat. I want to cry for us all, for the fact that the only hope that can be given to us is something that does its best to destroy us.

The woman closes her eyes, leans her head back and I force my gaze to the window where the cyclist is now gone, riding off to spend a couple of hours challenging his body, his healthy body, as I once had.

A nurse walks into the room, asks if she can do anything for anyone. I feel the response rising up out of me, like a tsunami wave cresting from the ocean floor. There is nothing I can do to stop it. "Yes," I say, the word emerging loud and adamant. "Take this out, please."

She walks over with a look on her face that says she has heard this before. "Now, Mr. Walker. You're not finished yet. It won't be too much longer."

"I am finished," I say.

She smiles an indulgent smile, turns and walks away. "It'll be over soon."

Rage flows over me in a red wave. I stare at the needle in my arm, and I know I'm done. I lift the tape that secures it above my vein, ignoring the instant pinch and yank it from my arm. I stand and leave the flowing tube of poison dripping onto the chair seat.

The woman next to me opens her eyes then, looks at me with approval, and I leave the room with a roar of anger choking in my throat.

Chapter Seven

"I'm not 40, I'm 18 with 22 years of experience."
– Unknown

Catherine

THE ENGLISH BREAKFAST buffet is everything it has been billed to be. It's set up in the beachfront Bajan Blue restaurant. As the hostess leads me to my table, I let my gaze take in the incredible scene before me. Blue, blue sky serves as a canopy to the blue-green ocean water, white sand beach and dozens of pink umbrellas and beach chairs. It is the dead of winter in New York. The colors here are a visual feast, and I can only imagine that people who see this every day must have much higher serotonin levels than the average person. I honestly could look at it forever.

"Will this be okay for you?" the hostess asks with a smile, waving a hand at the table facing the beach.

"It's perfect," I tell her, pulling out my chair.

"Would you like coffee this morning?"

"Yes, please."

She asks for my room number, and I give it to her after which she tells me to help myself to the breakfast buffet.

Hungry from the kick-butt spin class, I head for the food. There's a bar with pitchers of fresh green juice. I reach for one and snag a glass of carrot as well. I take them back to the table and then fill a plate with two boiled eggs, sliced tomatoes, blueberries and mango.

I eat as if I haven't eaten in days. I can't remember the last time food tasted this good, and I sit back, sipping my green juice and letting my gaze take in the beauty of the surroundings all over again.

The birds here have to be the happiest I've ever seen. But then if I were a bird, this is where I would want to live. A small wren tiptoes across the marble floor, spotting a blueberry beneath a chair. He snaps it up and flies over to sit on a rail in wait for the next morsel.

So I'm forty today.

The reality of that hits me all over again. It's something I've dreaded, a number that looms on the horizon once thirty is in the taillights. I think about the class I just finished, and I'm pleased I kept up with the instructor's admittedly demanding goals.

Anders.

The name matches the man. Strong. Memorable.

Something flutters in my stomach, and I let myself visualize his face and that incredible body of his. How long since I felt attracted to a man? No one man since Connor. Not one in three years.

When Connor and I were married, I had noticed

men. I'm not a complete prude. But it was never something I acted on. Notice and move on. Married didn't mean dead. But it did mean committed. To me, it had anyway.

My thoughts skitter back to Anders. You'd have to be dead not to notice him. Six-three would be my guess. Dark brown hair, short on the sides, longer on top. Wavy. Blue eyes, thick lashes, a dark slash of eyebrows. Sun-kissed skin. And those arms. Wide shoulders. Defined biceps.

And how old is he? Late twenties? I blink once, breaking my trance. Is forty too old to fantasize? Maybe not. But that doesn't make it pointless. Which it is.

I finish my juice, pour some coffee from the silver French press into my cup and pull out the novel I'd stowed in my bag earlier. I haven't read a book in ages, and I make a resolution to restore in my life some of the things I'd once loved to do. I'd started this morning with a good workout. Next on the list, reading.

I run my fingers across the cover of the hardback novel. I've spent the past three years mourning a life that is gone. For good. Never going to come back. For the first time in a long, long time, I wonder what might lie ahead for me. What if I'm not destined to spend the rest of my years alone, working like someone who has nothing else to define her?

A man like Anders Walker surely has a waiting list for lovers, all fifteen years younger than me.

I'd never dream of trying to throw my hat in that ring, but maybe he's been put in my path to remind me I can feel things I never thought I'd feel again. That's a present in and of itself.

I take a sip of my coffee, letting my gaze settle on the peaceful setting before me once more.

Happy birthday to me.

Chapter Eight

"Sometimes, the simple things are more fun and meaningful than all the banquets in the world …"

— E.A. Bucchianeri

Catherine

ONCE I'VE FINISHED breakfast, I head for the room to put on my bathing suit and pack a bag for the beach. I jump in the shower, run a razor over my legs and under my arms, towel off and slather on sunscreen.

I open the drawer in which I'd stored my bathing suits. One piece or two? Admittedly, I'm not feeling like the bikini should be an option, but I'd like to get a tan with as few lines as possible, and besides, I don't know anyone here, other than Madeline. I don't think she'll care whether I'm looking bikini-ready or not.

And so I settle on a lime green one, thinking I'll look a lot better in it once I have a little sun. Right now, it's giving me a New York winter milky glow.

Sighing, I grab my book, stow a bottle of water and extra sunscreen in the hotel's complimentary canvas bag and head out of the room. I take the stairs to the main floor and follow the hallway to the beach entrance. As soon as I open the door and step out into the warm air, I'm again assaulted by the beauty of this place. Birds are still chirping and tweeting as if they live in paradise, which, of course, they do.

Ahead of me, people are already set up for the day in pink chairs, an ice bucket with Evian on small tables in between. The blue-green water pulls at me like a magnet.

When I reach the white sand edge, a beach attendant greets me with a welcoming smile. "I'm Thomas. First day on the beach?" he asks.

"Yes," I say. "May I get a chair?"

"Certainly, you may. Your room number?"

I give it to him, and he checks a paper on his clipboard. "Ms. Camilleri?"

"Yes, that's right."

"Excellent. The way this works is once I get you set up, that'll be your chair for the duration of your vacation. You can come back to the same spot each day, and I'll have it all ready for you. Any preference on location, and I'll see what I can do?"

"The front row would be nice, and I'd love an umbrella when I'm ready to opt out of the sun."

"Of course. Are you expecting anyone else?"

"No. Just me."

"In that case, I've got a spot in the middle, right up front. That sound good?"

"Perfect," I say.

"Follow me." He grabs a few towels and leads the way. I slip off my sandals, my feet sinking into the warm sand. It feels so good, as if I've reconnected with something I never realized I'd been disconnected from. I think of all the concrete in Manhattan, how few times I actually touch grass or dirt there. Never, actually.

"Here you go. This look okay?"

"Better than okay," I say, letting my gaze settle on the view that will be mine for the next two weeks.

He folds a towel around the chair cushion, places one at the top as a headrest. "If you'd like something from the beach or when you're ready to order lunch, just stick the sign under your chair in the sand, and I'll be right over."

"Wonderful. Thank you so much." I pull a ten from the wallet in my canvas bag and hand it to him.

"Thank you. Enjoy your day, Ms. Camilleri."

"You too."

He walks away, and I settle back in the chair, the big pink umbrella shading my upper body, my legs warming in the sun. I marvel again at the sight before me. The so-tempting water rolls into the beach on peaceful waves, the sun a blazing bulb in the nearly cloudless sky.

It's only ten o'clock and already eighty-five degrees. I'm suddenly overcome with the desire to get in the water. I walk to the hut at the end of the beach and ask for a float. The attendant there hands me a white one with the hotel's signature on the raised pillow. I walk back to the area where my chair is and tread out far enough to lie face down on the float.

I paddle to where it's a little deeper. The water feels incredible. I remember it now from my trip here ten years ago. I had loved it then, and I love it again. I can't remember the last time anything felt this good. I swim to the floating dock a hundred yards or so from the beach, hold on to the ladder while I put my float on top and climb up. I'm the only one out here, and I sit on the bench to one side, staring back at the beach, at the children playing by the water's edge, listen to the tinker of laughter floating up from the beach-long row of chairs.

The whir of a Sea-Doo sounds behind me, and I look over my shoulder to see a guy cutting up with the waves. He angles the machine perpendicular to the rise of water, then guns it. The Sea-Doo goes airborne and lands with a smack. The rider's fit body beneath the life vest looks familiar, and I realize it's Anders from Spin. He looks my way at that moment, as if my gaze has pulled his to mine. I start to glance away, but something stops me. A moment of brazenness in which I hold the look, daring him to do anything about it.

Which he does. Immediately.

What did I just do?

He points the Sea-Doo toward the platform, letting off the gas far enough away that he floats up, the engine off, reaching out a hand to stop the machine from bumping the platform. "So how was that English buffet?" he asks, smiling his wide, very-white smile.

"Incredible," I say. "Glad I worked out first though."

"Good to hear. And now you're hanging out on the swim platform by yourself?"

"Basking in the sun and a little me-time. I've had worse days."

"Well, I certainly don't want to interrupt that, but wanna go for a ride?"

"Is this what you do when you're not bullying guests into taking your class?"

He laughs. "Bullying? Is that how I came across?"

"It could be interpreted that way."

"Fine. Bullying for the greater good then."

"I'll give you that."

"Actually, I'm out here making this thing look appealing so guests will want to rent it. Hop on and help me out."

Okay, so I'm not immune to flattery, despite the fact that I haven't flirted with a man in so long I should probably Google it before trying it on my own. Still, sitting on a Sea-Doo that close to the man in question doesn't seem like a good idea. "Ah, I don't have a life jacket."

He opens the storage compartment at the front of the machine and pulls out an extra. "Here you go," he says, handing it to me. "Problem solved."

"Shouldn't I be paying for a Sea-Doo ride given that I'm a hotel guest?"

"Technically, but if you're assisting with advertising, we'll let it slide this one time."

I laugh, the sound as unexpected to my ears as it appears to be to his.

"You should do that more often," he says, his voice low and ridiculously, I do mean ridiculously, sexy.

"What's that?" I ask, the words coming out as if someone else is in control of them.

"Laugh. It transforms you."

We hold each other's gaze for a couple of moments before I finally admit, "It's not something I've been doing a lot of for a while now."

"Come on then. I'm going to make it my one goal today to make you laugh. Get you back in practice."

This is a bad idea. I know it, and yet, here I go, standing, sliding the life vest on, zipping it. Like a marionette whose strings are being pulled by an unknown force.

He pats the seat behind him, and I slide on, something low and warm igniting in my mid-section at the realization that he is mere inches from me. His back is smooth and sun-brown, shoulder muscles bulging. And he smells good. Like he took a shower at the spa after class.

He shows me where to hold on, both of us obviously ignoring the option of me holding onto him. I follow his instructions and slip my fingers through the strap on the seat. "Ready?" he asks.

"Ready."

He guns it, and we're off, blasting across the water, a scream freeing itself from my throat. He heads farther from the beach, falling in behind a very large yacht making its way up the Barbados coast. The name emblazoned across the side is *Happy Ending*. Its waves are enormous, and Anders weaves in and out of them, the Sea-Doo complying like a playful dolphin. As we bob along, Anders gets more daring, seeking out the larger waves.

"You good?" he calls back.

"I think so," I say, smiling even as I realize I shouldn't encourage him.

"Hold on!"

I see the wave coming, and it is huge. Without thinking, I wrap my arms around his waist and press my cheek to the back of his jacket, closing my eyes.

We go airborne, and it seems like we hang there for a full minute before we land on the water, and he guns it again, rocketing us forward.

I hear cheering and glance at the back of the yacht to see some teenagers standing by the rail, clapping and whooping.

Anders laughs, and I can't help it, I do too, feeling a euphoria that is like a high of its own. He turns and heads farther from the beach, not stopping until the water is a much deeper blue, more ambitious waves tossing us up and down.

"You're crazy," I say when he turns to look at me.

"Crazy can be fun," he says, smiling.

I can't deny it, but shake my head, sliding farther back on the seat since we've been jostled closer together. He stands, pivots toward me.

We face one another as the Sea-Doo bobs gently, bow to stern on the undulating waves. I resist the urge to slide back on the seat, his closeness igniting my skin so that I feel as if heat emanates from me in a visible cloud of steam. I force myself to stay still, as if to move is to give away the attraction.

"So what makes a beautiful woman like you fly two thousand miles to celebrate her birthday alone?"

There are many ways to answer the question. Flip? *So I'd have a chance of meeting a guy like you.* Depressed? *I don't really have anyone close enough to justify inviting them.* The truth? "I wasn't up to the surprise fortieth being thrown for me."

"Ah. You don't like parties."

"Sometimes. Just not this one."

"Nothing wrong with a solo vacation birthday present from you to you."

I smile, surprising myself. "It was probably selfish. The people in the office had gone to a lot of trouble."

"But was it what *you* wanted?"

I glance out at the horizon where the ocean meets the sky and shake my head, slowly, and admitting, "No."

"I guess that's the flaw in the surprise party ointment. The givers don't ask the guest of honor if it's what she wants."

"I could have pretended."

"Yeah. And been miserable. This seems like a better choice," he says, waving a hand at the pink chair-lined beach still in sight.

"I can't deny that. And besides, forty is a crossroads. Kinda wanted to look at that by myself."

"How you figure?" he asks, leaning back and folding his arms across his life vest to give me a long assessment.

"For all the obvious reasons."

"Have you looked in the mirror lately?"

"Yes, as a matter of fact," I say, laughing lightly. "Right before I headed for the beach."

"If you're what forty looks like, no need to be worrying about a crossroads."

"Easy for you to say. What are you? Twenty-one?"

"Now would I have had time to crack a career on Wall Street if that were the case?"

"I guess not. Doesn't mean you don't look it."

"Thirty-one," he says. "Glad to hear my fitness regimen is working."

I raise an eyebrow in surprise. "I'll say."

He leans back. "Why, ma'am, are you flirting with me?"

"Hah! I was just thinking I'd need to do some research before trying that particular move out."

"So you were *thinking* about flirting with me?" He pulls his phone out of the compartment beneath the steering wheel, taps the screen, starts typing. "How to flirt with a younger man."

I smack his life jacket. "Stop!"

He holds the phone out of my reach. "Let's see. 14,700,000 results. Quite the popular topic we've stumbled into."

"Put that away," I say, smiling in spite of myself. "And quit flattering yourself."

He slips the phone back in the storage compartment, levels me with another steamy stare. "I would be flattered."

"Okay. You need to quit. Besides flattery isn't good for you. It gives you a big–"

"Ego?" he interrupts me, and we both laugh until

I'm pretty sure I could have appendicitis judging by the pain in my side.

"Seriously, stop!" I say, holding up a hand. "Really. Or I'm going to have to swim back."

"You won't be there in time for dinner," he teases.

"So that's a bad idea," I admit.

"All flirting aside, is it all right if I show you something?"

"Ah, sure," I say, wondering what it could be.

"Okay," he says, standing on one leg to swing around and face forward again. He starts the Sea-Doo and hits the gas so hard that it lifts and dips to the left, causing me to grab onto his shoulders.

As the machine settles itself, I snatch my hand back as if I've touched a hot stove. I find the strap on the seat instead, anchor my fingers through.

He aims the Sea-Doo toward the hotel, and we slow and settle over the waves until we reach the no-wake zone where he idles to the rental area. "I just need to get something out of a cooler, and we'll be on our way."

I'm curious but decide not to ask, watching as he speaks to one of the guys obviously in charge of renting the boats and other water toys. The guy glances at me, smiles and nods. Anders walks over to the cooler sitting on the beach, opens the lid and pulls out what looks like a takeout box. Carrying it, he splashes through the water and climbs back on.

"That's Ernesto. I told him we'd be back in an hour. He hasn't had any takers yet today, anyway."

"Where are we going?" I ask, as he idles back through the no-wake zone.

"It's a surprise," he throws over his shoulder. And then he laughs. "Wait. Don't bail on me. This is a good surprise. I think you're going to like it."

I start to protest, but we're already sailing off over the gentle waves. My "I hate surprises!" gets caught in the wind and is gone.

He angles right, the coast line flowing by in splashes of color, pink bougainvillea, a red umbrella, a bright green wooden boat bobbing against an anchor. The sky is that incredible blue above us, and for a moment, I think I must have landed in a dream. Yesterday morning, I woke to a cold, gray winter New York day. It seems impossible that this day could exist on the same planet.

We drive for ten minutes or so, and Anders points the Sea-Doo toward a row of buoys bouncing gently on the water.

He eases to a stop, pops the front compartment, pulling out the box he'd taken from the cooler. He opens it, scoops out something I can't see. "Come on," he says, sliding into the water.

I give him a skeptical look. "What are we doing?"

"Trust me."

It's a ridiculous request. I don't know him. He could be planning to drown me. Maybe all the flirtation stuff was a lead-up. "Ah, I'm just now remembering my mother taught me not to talk to strangers. And here I am out in the ocean with you, trusting you don't have some sinister plan to do away with me."

"Hold on," he says, leaning back to give me a look. "First, I'm expecting you in spin tomorrow, and second, what I really want to do is kiss you right now, but since it's way too soon for that, come on. Let's do this."

He slides off the Sea-Doo, making a splash into the water. I'm still suffering from the shell-shock brought on by his last admission. Did he say kiss me?

"Come on!" he calls back, waving one hand in my direction, clutching a plastic bag in the other.

I could overthink this, find plenty of reasons to stay right where I am. But the water is a deep compelling blue, and the sun is shining down on my face, and I want to. I just want to.

And so I do.

I stand up, step off the side and do a knife dive straight into the ocean.

The life vest brings me up. Sputtering, I push my hair out of my face as Anders reaches for my hand and drags me along behind him, kick-swimming several yards out from the Sea-Doo.

He lets go of my hand, opens the plastic bag and pulls out something, tossing it in the water.

"Is that meat?" I ask, picturing sharks from miles away calling all their friends and swimming toward us in a straight line.

"Yeah," he says. "Watch what happens."

He tosses out another piece, and I barely suppress a small squeal of terror, voicing my fear. "Um, are there sharks in these waters?"

He looks at me and laughs, as if I have truly amused him. "Here comes my girl."

I look out to where he's pointing and spot the sea

turtle swimming at us from just beneath the surface, her face pointed straight at Anders.

"Oh my gosh!" I scream in delight.

Anders holds out the treat, and she swims right up to him. He drops it in the water and she whisks it up. "Against the law to touch them," he says.

I stare at her, stunned by how beautiful she is. "How do you know she's a she?"

"Adult males have a long tail. Adult females don't. And the girls have prettier faces. She's a Loggerhead." He tosses out another treat, and she swims a circle around us and dives for the snack. "They have been considered critically endangered for some time now."

"Why?" I ask, crestfallen, my gaze falling to the beautiful turtle a few feet away.

"Over-harvesting by man. For the meat, shell and eggs."

Hearing the words makes me feel sick. "It's really too bad God made us overseer. We're certainly doing a lousy job."

"Yeah, I can't imagine we're impressing him. In 1987, the University of the West Indies started the Barbados Sea Turtle Project to restore the populations. Hunting turtles or their eggs is illegal and comes with huge fines and jail time. The efforts are working, but it's a shame that man can be so thoughtless and selfish."

A knot has formed in my chest. "She's so free and perfect. I can't stand the thought of someone hurting her."

"Me either." We're quiet for a few moments, and

then he says, "Did you know they can migrate incredible distances? So I read this study where they put satellite transmitters on four Hawksbill turtles in Barbados during the nesting season to figure out where they migrated to. All four left Barbados after their nesting and went as far as Dominica, Grenada, Trinidad, and Venezuela."

"How many miles is that?" I ask, shocked.

"Two seventy at the farthest."

"That is truly incredible. Why do they go so far?"

"Foraging for the things they like to eat. The sad part is much of the territory they end up being in doesn't protect them as they are protected here."

"That's terrible."

"Yes. I wish I could tell this girl not to ever leave these waters."

"Please don't," I say, looking at her sweet face again, unable to imagine someone taking her life.

"They are amazing creatures. They imprint the place where they're born and come back twenty to thirty years later to lay their own eggs."

"That long? That's smarter than anything I've ever done."

Anders laughs. "Me, too. Since I've thoroughly unveiled myself as a sea-turtle geek, I'll leave you with one more fact. They are very careful where they place their eggs. Sea-water kills the developing embryos. And the temperature of the sand determines the sex of the embryos. If the eggs are closer to the tide line where the sand is cooler, the eggs will produce a male. If it's in the warmer sand, the eggs produce females."

"Wow. I'm going to buy a book on sea turtles. I want to know everything about them."

He smiles and nods once. "I was bitten by the same bug. They really are fascinating."

"Thank you," I say, looking at him and realizing I've underestimated him. He's way more than a pretty face. "This is the best birthday present I've ever gotten."

He snags my gaze, and we float alongside the turtle, something real and substantial hanging there between us. What on earth?

"We're out of treats," he says softly, and as if she knows exactly what he's said, the turtle turns and swims peacefully off in the opposite direction.

"Come on," Anders says, taking my hand and pulling me back to the Sea-Doo.

Once we're there, he climbs on the back and tells me to place my feet on the rubber edge. He takes my hands and catapults me up. The Sea-Doo tips crazily side to side, and I'm forced to grab his waist to hold on. It settles eventually, and I pull back, staring up at him.

"Wanna drive?" he asks with a risk-taker smile.

"Me? I've never driven one."

"You gonna wait until you're fifty?"

I give him another playful slap, realizing I'm acting like I'm in high school with all the slapping, giggling and staring. Good grief. "No. As a matter of fact, I'm not. I think I'll learn today."

"Outstanding." He unhooks the cord with the key from his life jacket and hands it to me. "Snap it through one of the loops on your vest. If you fall off, you want the key to stay with you."

"Fall off? Oh ye of little faith."

"I see how it is," he says, smiling.

It takes a little maneuvering for us to switch spots. He holds onto the seat, giving me the chance to scoot forward. Then, he spins back around and climbs onto the seat behind me.

"What was that game I played as a kid? You put your hands and feet–"

"Twister," he says, laughing.

"This is definitely that." It feels different to have him behind me, and it feels absolutely safe when he reaches his arms around me, placing a hand on top of my own as I hold on to the handlebar grips.

His breath is against my ear and the warmth of it spreads over me like candlelight.

"The right side is the gas," he instructs me, pumping his right hand against mine. "The left side is for hitting neutral or reverse."

I grip my hand tight around the throttle, pressing my thumb down on it. The Sea-Doo bolts forward. From behind me, Anders jolts backwards. He grabs onto my side and holds on with both hands as I increase the speed.

I skip along the waves, running perpendicular to them. Each time we hit a bump, the front of the Sea-Doo aims skyward, and it's as if I'm flying with the weightless free fall of a roller coaster dropping at a precarious angle.

Once I manage to smooth out my efforts, I press the throttle and take a sharp right to head further out on the ocean where the waves are wilder, banging into each other before they have the chance to reach the shore.

But just then, a wave crashes against the side of the machine. The sea water drenches us both, the salt instantly burning my eyes, the taste of it on my lips.

It's only when Anders' grip tightens around my waist that I realize something has gone terribly wrong. And then I'm landing headfirst in the ocean, the Sea-Doo turning off as I take the key with me.

I go under, and it's as if I will never stop sinking, but the life jacket regains its footing and shoots me back to the surface like a rocket headed for the sun.

As soon as I break the surface, I gasp for air and blink the water from my eyes. I jerk my head right and left in search of Anders, and then hear his voice behind me.

"Are you okay?"

I whip around, thankful to see that I haven't killed him. "Ah, sorry?" I say.

But he's laughing, as if I've given him the thrill ride of his life.

"I knew you had it in you," he says, swimming toward me.

"Death by Sea-Doo?"

He laughs again. "If you don't get thrown off, you're not going for it hard enough."

"Oh, is that how it works?"

"Sure is."

The Sea-Doo is some fifteen yards away, waiting patiently for us like a horse who has no idea how the rider ended up on the ground.

"First one back gets to drive," he says and takes off swimming.

"No fair! You got a head start!"

I give it my best, but of course he beats me, and to be honest, I'm happy to let him take over the driving. By the time I get there, he's already on board, reaching a hand out to help me climb on the back.

I place my feet on the rubber edge, and he takes my hand, quickly pulling me up again where I bump into his chest and grab onto his jacket to right myself. He stares down at me, and for a second I think it wouldn't be so bad to drown in those blue eyes.

"There's something I'd really like to do," he says in that low, lust-inducing voice of his.

I hear in my head the words he'd said in the water earlier. *What I really want to do is kiss you.* "What's that?" I ask, wondering if I sound as jumbled as I feel.

"I'd like to take you to dinner for your birthday tonight."

"You don't have to do that." Surely he's being nice.

"I want to do that."

"Are you sure?"

"Never been more sure of anything."

I smile and nod. "Thank you." He pulls his phone out of the storage compartment, taps the screen and says, "May I have your number in case we need to touch base?"

I give it to him, and as we find our spots on the Sea-Doo and head back up the coast, I'm still thinking about that kiss.

Chapter Nine

"A moment's insight is sometimes worth a life's experience."
— Oliver Wendell Holmes, Sr.

Nicole

DR. BAKER'S OFFICE is on the fifth floor of a high-rise in West Palm Beach. This is only the third time she's had an appointment with him, and her stomach drops as she steps out of the elevator, apprehension popping a fine sheen of sweat across her forehead and the back of her neck.

She knows that the job of a psychiatrist isn't to judge his patient, but she can't talk to him about her life and the choices she's made without waiting for that look of disbelief to cross his face. *You did that?*

And so she arrives at each appointment with a sense of dread that hangs over her like a heavy grey curtain.

She wipes a hand across her forehead and opens the office door, stepping inside and walking over to the check-in window. The receptionist is moderately cheerful, as if she knows patients are there for serious reasons and it would be inappropriate to look too happy to see them.

Nicole gives her name. The woman checks her insurance card and her contact info, then asks her to take a seat in the waiting room. She's the only one here, which is a good thing as far as she's concerned. She hates making eye contact with other patients because there's always some reluctant acknowledgment that each of them would pretty much rather be anywhere else.

She flips through a couple of magazines, uninterested in the lives displayed on the pages, perfectly dressed people with flawless complexions getting out of Ferrari's in Hollywood. She used to look at such pictures with envy. Those people had the world by the tail. They were the chosen ones. Tragedy never touched them. Everything they wanted appeared as if by magic at their fingertips.

She's old enough and far enough down the road of life to know this isn't true. Those people have affairs. Over-invest. Gain weight. Lose weight. Betray. Are betrayed. Get married. Get divorced. They experience all the same highs and lows as the rest of the world. But maybe people like to buy into the fantasy, that somewhere, for someone, life is perfect. Like a novel with a pink bow happy ending, suspension of disbelief required.

The door at the corner of the waiting room opens. A nurse steps out. "Miss Camilleri?"

Nicole glances up, puts the magazine on the end table and follows the woman in white down a hallway to Dr. Baker's office. She opens the door, waves Nicole inside.

Dr. Baker looks up and smiles a smile she would have ordinarily found contagious. But somehow, here, she is suspicious of such gestures. "Hello, Nicole," he says. "How are you today?"

She takes the chair across from his desk, puts her purse on the floor and clasps her hands in her lap. "I'm good. How are you?"

"Fine, fine."

He studies her for a moment, and she remembers what she dislikes about these sessions. She feels as if she is under a microscope, resists the urge to squirm under the scrutiny.

"Where did we leave off last time?" he asks softly.

"Um. We were talking about my sister's birthday."

"Ah, yes. It was–"

"Today, actually."

He leans back, makes a teepee of his fingers, lets a few beats of silence drop between them. "And did you get in touch with her?"

"I decided you were right. I sent her an email wishing her a happy birthday."

"And has she responded?"

"No," Nicole says quickly. "But I didn't expect her to."

"Did you say anything else in the email?"

"Just that I hope she'll forgive me someday."

"Good. And do you think she will?"

She shrugs, looks down at her hands. And then, in a low voice, "No. And as I've said, I don't blame her."

Dr. Baker is silent until Nicole lifts her head and looks at him. "Neither one of us knows if that will turn out to be true. The only thing we can affect is how you see what has happened. And how you choose to be shaped by it."

Nicole laughs a soft laugh. "I choose to be shaped?"

He nods. "Yes. It is your choice, really."

"The only choice that was mine was cheating with my sister's husband."

Again, if she intended to shock him with her words, he appears unfazed. "That was your choice as well, I agree. And based on everything you've said here so far, it is something you seriously regret."

"Regret doesn't erase pain though, does it?"

"No, it does not."

"And it doesn't change the fact that I am a horrible person."

"Nicole. You made a mistake. One action does not define us for a lifetime."

"I'm afraid this one does."

He sits back in his chair, folds his arms and studies her for several long moments. "The question you have yet to answer is the why. Why did you choose to have an affair with your sister's husband? As I have explained to you before, I believe that until we can identify the root cause of our actions, we are doomed to make some version of the same mistakes again and again."

"I won't be making this one again," she declares instantly.

"Maybe not exactly. But some version of it, yes, I believe you will. It's what we humans do."

Nicole bites her lower lip, wanting to snap her disagreement with him, but she doesn't allow herself. She keeps her voice deliberately even when she says, "I have never been successful at beating my sister at anything, and I certainly didn't beat her at this."

"So your relationship with your sister has been a competitive one?"

She lifts her shoulders, shakes her head. "There was never any competition. Catherine always wins. It's just the way it is."

"Does she see it that way?"

"I don't know. It doesn't matter if she does or not. It's true."

"Does she see herself in competition with you?"

"I doubt it."

"Did. . ." He stops, looks down at his notes. "Connor. Did Connor know about this facet of your relationship with your sister?"

"Not unless she told him."

"And you never implied this to him?"

Nicole considers his words, trying to figure out his angle. "Connor wasn't interested in playing me against my sister."

"What was his interest?"

"Sex, I believe."

If she had hoped to shock Dr. Baker with her blunt assessment, she can see she has not. But then again, he's most likely heard it all. And then some.

"At the beginning, did you think this was the extent of his interest in you?"

"I suppose this is the point at which I admit I am a romantic fool?"

"No," he says in a level voice. "I'm trying to understand what your expectations were."

"And what if I didn't have any?"

"I would be surprised."

"Sex can't be for the sake of sex?"

"It can be for some people. I don't happen to think you're one of those people."

"I don't mean to be disrespectful, but you don't know me, Dr. Baker."

"I know pieces of you."

She stares at him, daring for a moment to let him see behind the curtain she attempts to wear as her expression. "Then you know I'm not a very good person."

"I don't know that at all."

She scoffs. "Good people betray their sisters?"

"Is that how you see what you did?"

"Isn't that how you see it?"

"It doesn't matter how I see it."

"Doesn't it? Why else would I be here?"

"I hope you're here because you want to see yourself in a way that would make such choices in the future an impossibility."

She laughs a light laugh. "So I'm suddenly going to start liking myself so much that I'll be above hurting my sister?"

"I would rather see it as you reaching a point where you respect yourself too much to be taken advantage of."

She leans back, looks at him through narrowed eyes. "You think I was taken advantage of?"

"Yes. I do."

She laughs outright now. "What would make you think that?"

He's silent long enough to make her uncomfortable. "The fact that anyone who knows you as well as your brother-in-law almost certainly knew you would have known you have a low sense of self-worth."

The words strike her chest like nails from a carpenter's gun. The sting they leave in their wake is enough to rob her of words. Never before has she thought of herself as being taken advantage of. In fact, she has seen herself as the one who opened the door to what happened in her sister's apartment that night. Invited it somehow even though it had honestly never occurred to her until the moment he had leaned in and kissed her and the pizza box had slipped from her hands.

She wants to deny the doctor's assertion, feels the need to tell him he is wrong. But any response she's compelled to wave as a flag of objection, sticks in her throat, and she can think of nothing to say.

Deep down, in a place she doesn't want to look at, she wonders if he is right.

Because if she is honest with herself, truly honest, she cannot deny that she has always thought her sister, her family, would be far better off without her.

Chapter Ten

"Learn to enjoy every minute of your life. Be happy now. Don't wait for something outside of yourself to make you happy in the future. Every minute should be enjoyed and savored."

— Earl Nightingale

Catherine

SO HE CLEANS up amazingly well.

He's standing there in the open doorway of my room, looking at me as if he thinks the same might apply to what I've done with myself.

"Come in," I say, sweeping an arm inward, and adding, "I just need to add earrings, and I'm ready."

He follows me in past the dark wood closet and mini bar and into the bedroom. I walk quickly past the bed, as if the veritable elephant has appeared in the room, and lead him through the glass pane doors onto the terrace. "Make yourself comfortable," I say. "I'll just be a minute."

He sits on the small sofa near the rail, instantly

dwarfing it. "Our reservation is at 7:30. I'm early. No hurry."

I head for the bathroom. I close the door and stare at my face in the mirror. Did I look like this when I arrived yesterday? I have an instant flash of the tired, sun-starved face I'd studied in this same mirror last night before going to bed. No. I had not looked like this. Not. At. All.

My cheeks are flushed, my eyes bright. There's color in my lips, as if all the blood has rushed there like they're waiting to be kissed.

Ridiculous!

I call myself on the fantasizing. That is absolutely all it could be since I am having dinner with a man nine years younger than I am who lives on an island in a permanent state of vacation. And looks like he walked out of a cologne ad in a men's magazine. Could that be any more different from my regular life?

No. I repeat: no.

I grab the earrings from the jewelry case I'd stowed in a side drawer, practice patience as I pop off the back and slip the stud through my ear.

This is not a date. Repeat after me, Catherine. *This is not a date.*

I draw in a reservoir of air and walk back to the terrace, putting in place my most convincing platonic smile.

At my entrance, he stands. "Before I told you how beautiful you look, I wanted to see if the earrings made a difference." He leans back and gives me a long surmisal. "Nope. You were beautiful before the earrings. But I like them. Can't go wrong with diamonds."

I laugh softly, feeling my cheeks light up with heat. "Thank you. I'm ready whenever you are," I say, suddenly sorry we have to walk through the bedroom again.

"After you," he says.

I lead the way across the marble floor, deliberately ignoring the bed and the fact that it suddenly seems enormous.

"Looks comfy," Anders throws out behind me.

"It is," I say, grabbing a shawl from the chest of drawers. "I mean for sleeping, that is."

Without missing a beat, he says, "What else would you be using it for?"

"We'd better hurry," I say, heading for the door. "Don't want to be late."

I hear him laughing as I click down the marble stairs, holding onto the rail as I go.

"Hold up there," he says. "We have plenty of time."

"Oh, I think it's better not to be late."

He catches up with me, still smiling.

"Stop," I say.

"What? It's just too tempting to tease you."

"Forty-year-olds aren't teasable."

"To the contrary, I find you very teasable."

Again, I try to ignore him. "So tell me where we're eating."

"She's ignoring me."

"You're impossible."

"Oh, I'm very possible."

"I need a drink. A large one."

"And she shall have a drink. Promptly." Still smiling, he takes my arm and turns me down the hall leading to the center of the hotel.

We arrive at the entrance to L'Acajou where a maitre'd greets us. "Mr. Walker. Ms. Camilleri. So happy you could join us this evening. We have a perfect table for you with an ocean view."

He leads the way through the restaurant with its colorful chair cushions and immaculately set tables. He holds out my chair and waits for Anders to sit before he leans down and says something close to his ear.

He then hands us each a menu and says, "Kyle will be your server this evening. He'll be right over."

"Thank you," Anders says, opening his menu.

"What was that?" I ask, curious about the silent exchange.

Anders smiles. "I bartend here in a pinch. He was just asking if his discretion was working."

"Was it?"

"Quite well, actually. I feel like a guest."

I smile and shake my head. "I would imagine it's far more entertaining to be you here than it is to be a guest."

"Is there a compliment wrapped up in there somewhere?"

"Maybe a small one."

"All right then. I'll take that. Now how about that drink?"

"What do you recommend?"

"That would be a rum punch if you're going for

an island favorite. One of sour, two of sweet, three of strong, four of weak. Lime, sugar, rum and water."

"Are you hoping to get me drunk?"

He raises an eyebrow. "Now do I look like the kind of guy who would–"

"Let's not answer that. I'll have a rum punch."

Our waiter appears at that moment, as if prearranged, asking us if he can bring us something from the bar. Anders orders two rum punches, and while we wait, I glance at the menu.

"Um, you don't have to actually buy my dinner," I say. "It's very–"

"Expensive. What? You think I left Wall Street because I wasn't any good?"

I hear the feigned hurt in his voice and tip my head. "No. It's just–"

"I'm old school. I invite you. I pay."

"I didn't mean to be rude."

"You weren't. Some traditions are kind of nice as they are though."

Hard to argue with that, so I don't. The waiter returns with our rum punches on a small tray. They look amazingly appealing. He sets them down in front of us and says he'll give us a few minutes to consider the menu.

I take a sip of my punch. "Um. Delicious. But I understand the three of strong. Whoo."

"It's a sipper."

"But it's so good," I say, taking a longer sip than the first one.

"Hey, now. Remember that getting you drunk thing."

"Actually, I don't get drunk."

"How you figure?"

"I never drink enough to get drunk."

"Don't say never until you've finished a rum punch or two."

"I promise not to embarrass you," I say, smiling.

"You might not get drunk, but I don't get embarrassed."

"Oh, really," I say, taking another sip of the punch which by now has spread a very nice warmth from my midsection up my chest and down each of my arms. "Nothing ever embarrasses you?"

"Nope."

"How is that possible?"

He shrugs. "Because I own my choices. I decided at some point along the way not to care if another person doesn't approve of my choice. I need to know that I think it's the right choice."

"But me getting drunk wouldn't be your choice?"

He smiles, shakes his head. "No, that would be your choice. Why would that embarrass me?"

The waiter appears at our table, asks if we're ready to order.

"Hold that thought," Anders says. And then, "What will you have?"

I open the menu to refresh my memory. Smiling at the waiter, I ask, "May I have the mushroom risotto and the sweet potato fries?"

Anders orders the sea bass and mushroom fricassée.

When the waiter heads for the kitchen, Anders picks up his phone and starts typing, saying out loud, "How to get to know someone on a date."

"Are you Googling that?"

"Oh. Here we go. 200 questions to get to know someone."

"Are we staying for breakfast as well?"

"Question number one. If you didn't have to sleep, what would you do with the extra time?"

"That's easy. Write a book."

"So you like to read?"

"I love to read. I don't make enough time for it."

"Favorite books?"

"Hmm. Books that make me think. Man's Search for Meaning. Viktor Frankl. How to Win Friends and Influence People. Dale Carnegie. And The Omnivore's Dilemma. Michael Pollan. That one made me a vegetarian."

"So you're really excited about that Sea Bass I just ordered."

I shake my head, smiling. "It's what you said before. I own my choices. You own yours."

"Touché."

"What's question number two?"

He glances at his phone screen. "What's your favorite piece of clothing ever?"

"Favorite piece of clothing. Let's see. Ah. A purple velvet hat I had in third grade. I was convinced it made me the next Drew Barrymore."

"Purple velvet, huh? If that choice didn't embarrass you–"

"Hand me that phone," I say, reaching out to snatch it from him. "Question number three. What job would you be terrible at?"

"Sumo wrestler," he says without hesitation. "The outfit would be the deal breaker. Thong. Me. No."

I laugh, bending over and holding my stomach.

"You're picturing it, aren't you?"

"I'm sorry. I-"

"Thought so. How would that go over in spin?"

I cover my mouth, trying to stop the laughter from spilling out. "What a wedgie that would-"

Now he's laughing. "Next question," he says, taking the phone back. "What's something you like to do the old-fashioned way?"

I hesitate long enough that he raises an eyebrow and smiles that suggestive smile of his. My heart ka-thumps a beat, and with a straight face, I say, "Talking on the phone instead of texting."

He's still smiling when he says, "Good one. Me too. So I read this article that said people are using texting to argue about issues in their relationship. This UCLA professor found that body language makes up fifty-eight percent of communication. Thirty-five percent is through body language and vocal tone. Seven percent was from the actual message."

"How scary is that? People say things in texts they would never say face to face."

"True that." He taps something onto the keyboard.

My phone dings from inside my clutch purse. Keeping my gaze on his, I pull it out and read the message on the screen. *You look incredibly hot tonight.*

I draw in a deep breath and reach for my rum punch, this sip not exactly a sip.

He holds my gaze, smiling.

Fortunately, the waiter arrives with our dinner, and I'm saved from a response. Not that I would have one.

The food looks incredible, and I'm suddenly famished. We pick up our forks at the same time, eating in cautious silence. We both murmur polite comments about the excellence of the food but otherwise finish our meal in silence.

"That was so good," I say, finally sitting back in defeat. "I can't finish though. I hate to waste it, but I'm so full."

He pushes his own plate back. "Think I'll leave a little myself. We aren't going to impress anyone with our dancing if we have huge bellies."

"What?"

"Dancing. Step two in our celebration of your birthday."

"You don't have to do that. This is more than enough."

"I want to do that." He waves a hand at the waiter. "This was wonderful," he says when the waiter arrives at the table. "But we've got a dance floor waiting on us."

"By all means," the waiter says. "I'll get the check."

Chapter Eleven

"The job of feets is walking, but their hobby is dancing."
— Amit Kalantri

Catherine

WE LEAVE THE hotel in a white van taxi. It weaves and winds the narrow Barbados roads, headlights flashing us from the right lane.

"Where are we going?" I ask, aware of the minuscule amount of distance between Anders and me on the seat behind the driver.

"Red Door," he says. "Best club on the island."

"Ah, there's something I need to tell you."

"Let me guess. You don't dance?"

"How did you know?" I can still hear the rum punch in my voice, the way it adds a lilt to the ends of my words.

"As of tonight, your first night of being forty, you dance. Just like you now drive a Sea-Doo."

"Then surely you know you will regret this."

"Remember? I don't embarrass."

"So you're owning the choice of taking me out dancing?"

"Damn right I am," he says, throwing me a grin.

Realizing I've defeated my own argument, I sit back and watch night-cloaked Barbados roll past my window, wondering if I will be the first reason ever Anders Walker has to be truly mortified.

*

ONE OF THE HOUSE specialty drinks is the Red Door Mule.

As it turns out, the Red Door Mule is all you need to become an incredible dancer.

Or at least, to make you *think* you're one.

I've had two, and I'm pretty sure that's my limit, but I'm dancing. I feel liquid, free and ridiculously happy.

The dance floor is so crowded I'm all but pressed right up against Anders. Who happens to be one of the best dancers I've ever seen. I mean like he could be on Dancing to the Stars. I mean with. *With* the Stars.

His body loves the music. And I love his body. I love *watching* his body. I'm not even thinking about my own moves. I'm just following the beat, completely mesmerized by the man in front of me.

There isn't an insecure bone in him. The music just becomes part of him. We're two in a crowd of swaying, laughing, happy people, the music a pounding pulse in our ears, the beat deep and contagious.

Someone jostles into me from behind, and I tip forward, falling into Anders with a gasp. "Easy there," he says, his head dipped low to my ear as he loops an arm around my waist and pulls me flush against him.

I look up, our gazes locked and searing.

I'd forgotten what physical attraction feels like.

But I am remembering. In every fiber of my being, I am remembering. It's as if there is a magnet inside each of us, and we're being pulled to each other at the cellular level. Our bodies dip and weave beneath the throb of the music, and I'm really hoping he never takes his arm away, never lets me go. Beneath the silk of my dress, I feel the hard sculpt of his thighs and yet further proof that all those hours on the bike have turned him into a living work of art.

A waiter brings us two more drinks, setting them on a nearby table. Anders takes my elbow and leads me over.

"My last one," I say. "No more mules for me."

Anders shakes his head, smiling. "Have you seen that uptight New Yorker I took to dinner earlier?"

"Uptight?!? Oh, wait. I was a little uptight about turning forty, wasn't I? Didn't someone say age is of no importance unless you're a cheese?"

He laughs. "Or a bottle of wine."

"I'd rather be a forty-year-old bottle of wine than a forty-year-old cheese."

"For the aroma alone," he agrees, taking another sip of his drink.

I giggle and pull him back to the dance floor.

"So you like dancing?" he teases, reeling me in

again and putting me back in the very spot I wanted to be in all along.

"I don't think I'll remember in the morning how bad I am! And don't remind me."

"I like watching you move," he says, dipping his head low, and grazing my cheek with his lips.

It's as if I've had an arrow of desire shot through my center, and I'm thinking I am in serious trouble.

I'm not sure how long we stay in the middle of the throbbing throng of people, six songs, seven? My dress is clinging where sweat dampens my skin, but even so, I'm not ready to leave the dance floor when the song ends, and his arm drops from my waist. I'm disappointed when he leans in and says, "Let's get some air."

He takes my hand and leads me through the crowd, dodging dancers until we walk through a door and into the cool of the night.

People are waiting in line to get inside, and we find a spot in the shadows of the building. Anders leans against a wall, arms folded across his chest. "Girl can dance."

"Not compared to you," I say, laughing softly. The sky swirls above me. "I think that Red Door Mule has a pretty good kick."

He smiles. "Also thought you didn't get drunk."

"I'm not drunk." Did the n in drunk slur? "And you have to stop."

"Stop what?"

"This . . . this flirting with me. It's like . . . like holding a glass of water out to a woman who's just walked through the desert when you have no intention of *giving* the water to the woman."

Anders smiles, tips his head. "Who says I'm not going to give her the water?"

"Well . . . you can't. You're young. She's old. And the water won't do her any good anyway. It's too late. She's all dried up," I say, shaking my head and then forcing myself to go still since the sky just dipped toward us again.

He's staring at me with the kind of heat in his eyes I've never had directed at me quite so intently.

"Baby, it's never too late," he says. With the quickness of a lightning strike, he swoops in, kissing me so long and with such deliberate expertise that I can't breathe. I *really* can't breathe. And maybe I don't want to if it means he has to stop. He's the stray bolt from the sky, and I'm the ground, and there's definitely an explosion going on here that demands life-saving action. I slide my arms around his neck and hold on, for dear life, actually, and while I'm at it, I kiss him back. Not with any kind of expertise, mind you. I'm so out of practice that without the muscle-relaxing effects of the alcohol I've consumed this evening, I'm pretty sure I'd be stiff as a board.

But, oh my gosh, he feels so good. And he *tastes* so good. I open my mouth beneath his, and we set about devouring one another, kissing like we're oxygen-starved and the only place to find air is here in this life-inducing act of passion.

I anchor my hands to his shirt and tip my head back. His mouth leaves mine, and he traces a path along my jaw and down my neck to the hollow at the center of my neck. From there to the crest of my breast at the neckline of my dress.

"We're going to need that water now," I say. "We seem to have started a small fire."

His laugh is explosive. "You're incredibly funny," he says, staring down at me now with smoldering blue eyes.

"Me? No. I'm not funny. I've never been funny. I'm serious. Serious people aren't funny."

He laughs again. "Okay. You can't dance. You never get drunk. And you're not funny. Quite a list we've got going here."

I angle back, give him a long look that admittedly goes a little fuzzy around the edges.

"I'd better get you back to the hotel before that mule knocks both of us out."

"Party pooper," I say, hanging back when he takes my hand.

He looks at me then, shakes his head and chuckles.

Chapter Twelve

"Some people believe holding on and hanging in there are signs of great strength. However, there are times when it takes much more strength to know when to let go and then do it."

— Ann Landers

Anders

WE END UP on the beach once we get back to the hotel.

The non-partying, non-dancing woman I took to dinner doesn't want the night to end.

If I'm honest, neither do I.

From the center of the hotel, we go left, away from the lights. Catherine runs to the edge of the water, splashing in to her knees, a wave smacking the front of her dress. She screams, laughing, and jumps back, promptly falling in the sand onto her delectable butt. Gentle waves lap around her hips and thighs, and I find myself envying them.

"I'm not sure silk and sea water are a good

combination," I say, reaching out a hand to help her up. She takes it, and just as I'm about to pop her out of the sand, she gives me a tug and I nearly fall on her, rolling to avoid her.

She's laughing now, and even though I'm wearing a jacket and pants, I don't bother trying to save them. I lie back and stare at the moon hanging bold and full in the night sky. "I'll send you my dry-cleaning bill."

She rolls over, hooks an arm across my chest. "I'm sorry. Very. Very, very sorry."

The apology is hi-jacked at the ends by the combination of Red Door Mules and rum punch. Her face is poised above mine, and I'm pretty sure I'm not coming into focus. "That's a lot of verys," I say.

"Oh, sorry. Not very. Just sorry."

I laugh. "See. You're a funny drunk."

"I'm not drunk," she protests, raising up to glare down at me. Her elbow slips, and she's suddenly flat on my chest. I take advantage of the moment to seek her mouth again since I haven't stopped thinking about that kiss since we left the Red Door. All the way back in the taxi. And all the way through the hotel lobby and out to the beach. Now when I'm wondering if I could actually ever get enough of her.

She kisses me back, and we're alone out here with the gentle lap of waves as our soundtrack. Catherine slides on top of me, and there's no mistaking when she takes over the kissing initiative. I lie back and enjoy it, not bothering to hide the fact that my body wants her. At this point, my brain's not talking the rest of me out of it, anyway.

If I've ever wanted to freeze-frame a page of my life, this would be the night to do it. I have a beautiful woman on top of me, a woman I admired before I left Wall Street. A woman who built a business from the ground up and made it into something other people were willing to pay a lot of money for. But she's not anything like I would have imagined her to be.

She makes a soft sound of protest and lifts her head. I want to protest the removal of her mouth from mine, but instead I run my hands down the back of her dress and under it to her sand-covered thighs.

"Um," she says, looking down at me again. "Better stop that."

"Now you're the party pooper."

"You. Are such. Trouble."

I smile and take my hands away. "See how easy I am."

"I think I'm going to be the easy one if I'm not careful. I need to go for a run."

She stumbles to her feet, trots a few yards away and takes off in a sprint.

"Wait!" I call out, getting up to run after her. "Catherine!"

I have no idea where she got the energy but it takes me a good thirty seconds to catch her. I scoop her up with one arm and swing her toward me. "Hey now, it's a little dark to see where you're going."

"I can see."

"Really?" I ask, looking up at her because I'm holding her against me with my arms locked beneath the butt I very much want to sink my hands into.

"Really."

"You don't sound sober."

"I am sober. Very, I mean incredibly sober."

Suddenly, I realize that she's crying. A tear drops on my face, and I ease her to the sand. "Hey. What's wrong?"

She looks down, shakes her head. "Nothing. I-" Her voice breaks, and she goes silent.

"I thought we were having fun."

"We were. Am. Are."

"Tears aren't the thing that makes a guy think you're having a good time."

"I'm sorry. I never expected tonight to-"

"What?"

She's quiet for long enough that I don't think she's going to tell me.

And then in a fast voice, she says, "I spent my honeymoon with my husband at this hotel."

I admit this isn't what I expected. "Husband?"

"Ex. Husband. We made out on the beach like you and I were-"

I feel as if a tsunami wave has just risen from the ocean floor and crashed down on top of me. "Ah. I get no points for originality then."

"No. You were very original. It just . . . brought back memories I'd rather forget."

I run a hand through my hair. "How long ago was that?"

"Ten years."

"How long have you been divorced?"

"Three."

"Mutual break-up?"

"Not exactly."

She drops onto the sand, pulling her knees up against her chest and staring out at the moon shining on the ocean's surface. "He had an affair with my sister."

The words appear out of the night, and it takes me a second to realize exactly what she said. "Oh. That-"

"-means there must really be something wrong with me."

"Whoa," I say, putting a hand on her arm. "That means there's something wrong with the two of them."

"Who does that?" she asks. "Even if I did have Grand Canyon size flaws. Who does that?"

I put a hand on her arm, pressing softly. "Hey. You don't have to open all this up."

"It's never closed," she says, the words barely audible.

I slip my arm around her shoulders and pull her up against me. "You know as well as I do there aren't any words of comfort in the whole Oxford dictionary to address this one. How about I just hold you?"

She drops her head on my shoulder, and we sit there, silent and bonded. I don't even know how it happened so quickly. We just met, but I feel it, and it grabs me deep down in the gut. I feel her hurt. It's like something real and tangible that's formed in the air between us.

She relaxes into sleep. Her head droops a little, and her breathing deepens. I'm almost glad. At least sleep has the ability to steal the pain of those memories.

I wait a couple of minutes to make sure she's completely out. I angle my body slightly away from her, stand and manage to slip my arm around her waist. I lift her in a single swoop. I know she can't weigh more than a hundred and twenty pounds at five-seven or so, but Catherine asleep is a lot more than one-twenty. And I'm really hoping that room key is in the small clutch purse still draped across her shoulder and no doubt filled with sand.

I head for the walkway between the hotel and the beach. I step up, holding onto her tighter. The last thing I want to do is stumble and drop her.

When I get to the door that leads to the guest rooms, I reach two fingers out and pull the handle. I determine not to slip on the marble and walk straight for the staircase that leads to the third floor.

I admit to being out of breath when we get there, spin instructor or not.

Still holding her in my arms, I fumble for the small purse I am really hoping holds her room key. I turn the twist latch and slip my hand inside. Sand. Lipstick. Breath mints? Card key. Yes.

I pull it out, slide it in the lock, realize I've inserted it the wrong way and try again. The light on top of the lock flashes bright green, and the door clicks open. I shoulder it in and step quickly inside, even as it swings shut behind me.

I head straight for the bed, glad that housekeeping has already provided turn down service. I lean in and place her gently on the covers. I don't see her waking up to change clothes. Which means she'll have to sleep in the sandy dress because me helping her out of it would be crossing a line I'm not going to cross.

Me, on the other hand? I'll sleep in the chair, but the clothes have to go.

Chapter Thirteen

"If you're going to do something tonight that you'll be sorry for tomorrow morning, sleep late."
– Henny Youngman

Catherine

OH. MY. GOSH. My head hurts.

I open my eyes and try to remember where I am.

I literally feel as if I've been kicked in the head by a mule. Which, I guess, by any realistic consideration, I have. Three times, actually. And that's not counting the rum punch.

The blackout curtains fail to contain the strip of sunlight stealing its way into the room.

My eyes adjust to the dimness, and I suddenly realize I'm not alone. I bolt up against the pillow, fear flooding my veins so quickly that I am lightheaded with it.

My feet are on the floor when I see that it is Anders.

Sleeping in the chair. His head cocked to one side

in what looks to be a very uncomfortable position. And he's wearing the white hotel robe from my closet.

I glance down to see what I'm wearing.

The dress I wore to dinner. And, oh my gosh, where did I get all this sand?

The sheets are gritty with it. I put a hand to the back of my hair and find it there as well.

A fuzzy recollection of me, on the beach, pulling Anders down into the sand. Oh. Dear. Heavens.

Heat floods my face at the memory. Embarrassment and something else too. I feel the weight of him on top of me, his mouth sinking onto mine.

I make a dash for the bathroom, close the door and lock it.

My phone is on the sink with enough battery life left to reveal the time as six-thirty. I consider waking Anders since he has to get to his class, but I can't face him without a shower first. I turn on the water and step inside before it warms up, blasting myself with the cold spray and gasping even as I admit I deserve it.

I stand still until the water turns warm and then let it sluice the sand from my body and my hair. If mortification has a theme song, it has opened a club in my head, its beat pounding out a rhythm I am sure I will march to all day long.

I've dragged the shower out as long as I should. There's no avoiding an encounter with Anders. Might as well get it over with. Walk of shame coming right up.

I get out, towel off and slip on the white robe hanging on the door. I run a comb through my hair and drag my feet to the bedroom, calling his name to wake him up.

But as my eyes adjust to the dimness, I see that the chair is empty. And he is gone.

*

I ORDER COFFEE and bring myself fully awake now, sitting on the balcony and staring out at the ocean where the waves are tame this morning. The sun is up, tinting the sky with pink. And the birds are singing their songs of happiness, sometimes solo, sometimes in unison.

I've finished my third cup before I cease the self-flagellation, grateful that Anders had let himself out.

It would be hard to blame him for wanting to avoid an uncomfortable exit.

I try to remember everything I said to him when we were on the beach, and there are some definite blanks. I would very much like to kick myself.

I could hide out in the room all day. Take every precaution to make sure I don't run into Anders Walker again. Which won't be easy, true.

Or check for an afternoon flight back to New York.

I give both options a good bit of consideration before I dismiss each of them.

I hear my phone ring through the crack in the doors between the bedroom and the balcony.

When had I turned it back on? I have no idea.

I could ignore it. But I don't. I get up and grab it

from the nightstand by the bed. It's a FaceTime call, and I click on the icon, James's face filling my screen.

"Oh, thank God, you're alive," he says.

"Sorry," I say, trying to sound as if I really am. "I should have told you where I was going."

"You think?"

"I know," I admit on a sigh.

"What the heck, Catherine?"

"I wanted to turn forty alone."

"You knew about the surprise party?"

"I got wind of it."

"I figured."

"How was it?"

"A blast, actually. We set a picture of you in the center of the food table and sang happy birthday to it."

A laugh sputters out of me. "You did not."

"Did too. No point in wasting a good catering."

"I'm sorry. Really."

He shrugs. "I should have asked you if you wanted the party."

"If I weren't such a control freak-"

"You wouldn't be CEO of ActivGirl."

"I'd have a lot more friends though."

"You have me."

"And I need to do a better job of showing how much I appreciate that."

"You show it. I liked my last bonus."

"Mercenary."

"Hey, a guy's gotta eat."

"You do eat well."

"So what'd you do last night? Blow out your candles alone?"

"I didn't have any candles."

"No one should spend their fortieth by themselves."

"Actually . . . I didn't."

He sits up in the desk chair. "You didn't?"

"I went out to dinner."

"With someone you met there?"

I shrug, nod once.

"Well, all right. It's about time."

"Oh, don't get too excited. After I got drunk and made a fool of myself on the beach, I'm sure he'll do his best to avoid me."

"I've never seen you drunk. Are you a fun drunk or a mean drunk?"

"A sloppy drunk, I'm afraid."

"Sloppy can be fun," he says.

"Or just plain embarrassing."

"I'm glad you decided to take this trip, Cat. It's definitely time to see what else is out there for you. Life needs to go on."

"He was just being nice because it was my birthday."

"Nothing wrong with that." He hesitates, and I can see there's something he wants to say.

"What is it, James?"

"Your sister called yesterday and tried to get me to tell her where you are. Of course I didn't know at the time so I couldn't tell her, but she seemed upset. And very much wanted to talk to you."

"Did she say why?"

James shakes his head. "And I would ask where you are, but if you don't tell me, I can't accidentally let it slip."

"Should I come back?" The question is out before I realize I even intended to ask it.

"No," he says immediately. "We got this here for now. You do some you time. It's long overdue. If anything catastrophic looks like it's going to happen, I'll be the first to call you."

Part of me wants to protest, insist that I should just get back to real life because we both know this isn't me. Even so, I don't want to leave just yet. Something about this place makes me want to forget about the life I've made in New York and the never-ceasing demands of an always hungry to grow business.

"Okay," I say. "I'll leave my phone on for the rest of the trip."

"That much I will ask of you. I've been in a state of panic."

"I'm sorry."

"Just unwind and come back to us revved up and revived."

I smile, even as my stomach dips at the thought of the workload that will be waiting for me. "Tall order. I'll try."

We click off, and I'm newly grateful for my assistant and his loyalty. We genuinely like each other, and I think we would even if we didn't have a working relationship.

I glance at the clock on the nightstand. Too late to

opt in for spin even if I could find the courage to face Anders.

A run is what I need. A good sweat and something to focus on aside from my stinging conscience.

Chapter Fourteen

"Did I do that?"
— Steve Urkel

Anders

I'M JUST LEAVING the spa still dressed in my workout clothes when I spot Catherine headed up the driveway away from the hotel. She's running at an impressive pace, given the fact that I'm pretty sure she has to have a banger of a headache this morning.

I take off jogging in the same direction, not wanting to look like I'm chasing her. She's passed the gatehouse at the main entrance and crossed the road to the residential street that winds up past the tennis courts by the time I catch her. I call her name, but she keeps going. I jog up beside her, tapping her on the shoulder when I realize she has headphones in and hasn't heard me.

She jumps and screams. "You scared me!" she says, a hand over her heart.

"Sorry," I say, holding up two hands in peace.

She bends, grabs her knees and pulls in air. When

she straightens, she shakes her head and says, "If you'd been a bus, I'd be dead."

I laugh. "That might be true. I thought you'd go back to bed."

"Yeah. That. I chose self-recrimination and sweat detox as more deserving options."

"Hey. It was your birthday."

She lets herself meet eyes with me then. "It was fun. Thank you. I'm just sorry I-"

I reach out a hand, touch her shoulder. "There's nothing you need to be sorry for."

"Not even the terrible dancing?"

"No."

"Assaulting you on the beach?"

"That was actually kind of fun."

The red in her cheeks darkens. "The counseling session where I drowned you in my romantic history?"

"Nope. Don't need to be sorry for that either."

"Thanks," she says again, obviously embarrassed. She hesitates, holds my gaze for a few beats, and then, "Would you be up for finishing this run with me?"

"Matter of fact, I'm all warmed up," I say, taking off up the hill at a sprint.

"Hey! No fair!" she calls out. "And why aren't you hung over?"

"Who says I'm not?"

"You don't look like it," she says, puffing between words.

I slow my pace, let her catch up. "There are some incredible houses along here."

"Are you changing the subject?"

"Just stating the obvious."

"Okay. Here's another obvious for you. I don't think I'm going to make it up this hill, beautiful houses or not."

I reach out, grab her hand and forge ahead. "Come on. No quitting now. You've still got that English buffet to earn."

"Oh. Don't mention food, please."

"Missed you in spin."

"Did not."

"Did too."

"I have a feeling I'm going to throw up before we're done here. I don't think the class would have appreciated that."

"You may have a point there."

The road flattens for a short stretch. "Oh, thank goodness," she says, wiping sweat from her forehead with the back of her hand.

"The view at the top will be worth it. I promise."

"Can we walk?"

"No. You'll thank me once you've reached your goal."

"Who says I had a goal?"

I laugh, picking up the pace again. "Come on. No talking until we get to the top. Focus on your breath."

"If I'd known you were wearing your trainer hat, I wouldn't have invited you."

"I'm not even going to charge you."

"Hah!" The laugh sputters out of her, and suddenly, she's bolting past me, headed up the next hill.

"Hey, wait for me!"

She laughs, but runs on as if I'm chasing her. I let her keep the lead because it seems like good motivation for her.

And it isn't until we reach the top where a view of the ocean sails out before us that she does exactly as she had predicted: drops to her knees and promptly throws up.

*

SHE IS MORTIFIED.

I'm pretty sure she'd like to make a rope of my sympathetic reassurances and hang me with it. A few minutes pass while she takes in air and regains her composure.

"Am I destined to humiliate myself in front of you?" she finally asks.

"Don't waste any energy worrying about that. I've paid the price for over indulgence more times than I'd care to admit."

"I've never done this. Ever."

"Then you were overdue. Everyone needs to lose control once in a while."

"Why?" she asks, leaning back to look at me with an incredulous stare.

"Because what control freaks fear most is losing control."

"How do you know I'm a control freak?"

"Aren't you?"

She'd like to deny it. The evidence is there on her face, the struggle between making an argument to the contrary and the realization that she's already given me plenty of evidence to support my assertion.

She shrugs. "Not that it does any good being one. Trying to control life is like trying to hold water in your hands. There's only so much that will fit in your palm. The rest is just going to leak out."

"Come on. Let's walk. Don't want to cramp up."

"More discomfort at this point really won't make a difference."

I put a loose arm around her shoulders and nudge her forward. "Yeah. It will." We walk a couple of hundred yards before I say, "So you're looking at a reformed control freak."

"You?" she asks, the doubt clear in her voice.

"I look way too laid back, right?"

"Well . . . yeah. Control freaks don't usually walk away from things like Wall Street."

"No. They don't. I was a perfectionist. Had to make straight A's in school. Graduate at the top of my class. Be among the top hires."

"That's great, isn't it? Impressive anyway."

"Yeah, if you actually appreciate yourself for those accomplishments. I couldn't do that because I was always looking for the thing I hadn't yet done and defining myself by that."

She's quiet, and I have to wonder if she's recognizing herself in what I've just said. "A counselor once told me the need to control is really about perfectionism and the inability to accept uncertainty. Do you agree with that?"

I glance out at the ocean to our right, stare at it for a few moments before I say, "I grew up in foster care, not knowing whether I would be in a different home from one week to another. And I guess my trying to create a life as perfect as I could make it was all about denying uncertainty."

"Oh. Anders. I didn't mean to pry-"

"It's okay," I say. "My mom was a teenager when she had me. Motherhood proved too hard at that point. She left me alone overnight when I was three and the state took me away from her."

She looks horrified. "I'm sorry."

I shrug. "That was part of my life. I can't deny it. I guess I've finally gotten to a place of accepting that all of that has made me who I am today. A man who accepts that there's little in this world that's for certain. At some point, I decided to take each day as it comes and try not to mold it in my image."

She stops, folds her arms across her chest and stares out at the ocean far below. "Do you ever see your mother?"

"She died when I was seven. I never knew who my dad was."

She looks at me, holds my gaze for several long moments. "That's an awful lot of uncertainty."

"It was. I tried to outrun it by trying to prove that the bad stuff can't touch you if you're perfect enough."

"I know what you had to do to get a job with that firm on Wall Street. After all that, you just found the courage to walk away?"

"There's a little more to it," I say.

"What?" she asks, caution entering her voice.

"We'll save that for another day," I determine, suddenly certain I do not want to change the way she sees me. Because I know that if I tell her the truth, she will not look at me the same. And I'm not ready for that yet. I suppose it's inevitable, but I don't want to see that look in her eyes. Not yet.

*

Four years ago

ONCE PEOPLE REALIZE you have cancer, they don't look at you the same. It's not that I blame them or don't understand the reaction. I do. If I'm honest, I can admit I've had the same feelings myself. Pity. Empathy. And there's fear too. Maybe all us are so afraid of getting it that on some level we're afraid it's contagious.

When someone looks the way I look now, it is an understandable fear. I am the poster boy for what cancer does to a human body.

I stare at my reflection in the bathroom mirror and realize I have given up on the only hope I've been given. Six weeks ago, I knew nothing about cancer. Nothing about treatment options other than the most obvious facts known to the public. What I know now is that conventional treatment will not be for me.

I go into my small living room that has not seen the touch of a decorator and is bare in the way of a place more passed through than lived in. A desk sits by the window that overlooks a busy Manhattan street. My laptop sits in the center, and I realize I haven't touched it in weeks.

For the first week of chemo, I went to work after the session. But as the nausea kicked in, and I was spending more time going to the bathroom to throw up, it became obvious there was little point to my being there. And so, I asked my manager for some time off. I couldn't give him any idea of how much time. I didn't know myself. I realize now I am never going back to that office.

I stand next to the chair beside the desk, study the people walking by below, joggers weaving their way down the sidewalk. A wave of weakness hits me, and I sink onto the chair, wondering if my body is telling me it is time to give up.

Some part of me wants to. I'm shocked by the thought. Two months ago, I would never have believed I could even think it. But it feels like the easy way. The road that won't require more struggle to find the will to fight. I glance at the bed visible through the bedroom door and wonder if I should just lie down and wait for death to take me. Stop eating. Stop drinking. Let the inevitable hurry toward me. Is that so unreasonable if that is where I will end up, anyway?

If there is an actual bottom for a person to hit, I realize that I am there. There is nowhere to look but up.

I reach out and lift the lid to my laptop. The screen lights up. Facebook is the window I'd last had open in the browser. I stare at the page, and I don't have the heart to scroll down the feed and see the undeniable evidence that the world is already going on without me. Birthdays being celebrated. New babies being born. Dogs being adored by their people.

As the wireless signal registers, the page refreshes, and a new post pops up in the feed. It's a picture of an infinity pool with a person standing at its edge. The water looks so inviting that I am captivated by it. I glance at the type on the picture and then read it. **Where Hope Lives.** The words settle for a moment, and I click on the photo. It takes me to the home page. Sanoviv Medical Institute. Curious, I read the recommendations of people who had been there. I quickly realize I'm reading about people like me, people on the verge of giving up. Who did not want to go the normal route of conventional medicine.

I click over to the website and read further. And for the next two hours, I lose myself in reading every piece of information available on the website and then I read every review and testimonial I can find.

By the time I sit back and close my laptop, I know that I am going to this place. I have absolutely nothing to lose.

Chapter Fifteen

"Of two sisters one is always the watcher, one the dancer."

— Louise Gluck

Nicole

Twenty-eight years ago

SHE CAN SEE that Catherine is going to have breasts before she does.

They're at Camp Wagamucha in North Carolina for a four-week stay away from home, the first time their parents let them go for this long. Their original intention had been to let only Catherine go, but Nicole had begged until they couldn't stand hearing her ask one more time and finally said, okay, you can go too.

The Camp Wagamucha T-shirt is the clue to Nicole's observation. Catherine's once flat-as-a-pancake chest is no longer flat at all, and the T-shirt does little to conceal the small but notable buds(they'd learned in health class that's what they were called ooh gross).

Even though she finds the whole idea nauseating in the same way she feels after eating too much popcorn at the movies, she still knows a pang of jealousy. She's only ten. Catherine is twelve, and Nicole can only begin to guess at all the things Catherine will start to want to do without her.

She really doesn't have any idea what those things will be but just the thought terrifies her. For as long as she can remember, as far back as her memory goes, she and Catherine do everything together. Where Catherine leads, Nicole follows. Their Grandpa's nickname for them was Pete and Repete. If it was good enough for Catherine to do, Nicole did not need to question it.

Sitting here now on the sandy beach made for the camp on Lake Wagamucha, Nicole would like to burn the eyes out of Johnny Atkins. He's been staring at Catherine's chest for the entire ten minutes they've been waiting for their canoes to be brought over from the storage dock. Or most of it anyway. And somehow, even though she doesn't think Catherine has noticed yet, she has a feeling she will like Johnny's attention when she does become aware of it.

Nicole steps in front of Catherine, blocking Johnny's view. "I want to ride with you, Cat," she says.

Catherine glances around, as if to make sure no friends have heard Nicole's heartfelt plea. "Don't you want to ride with Sarah and Penny?" she asks, her gaze skipping to Johnny. And it's then that Nicole knows she has been wrong. Catherine has noticed Johnny looking at her, and she's hoping he'll ask to ride with her in the canoe.

Nicole clutches her stomach and puts on her most pained expression. "My stomach hurts, Cat."

Catherine fails to hide the flash of irritation, but it is quickly replaced by concern. "What's wrong?"

"I don't know. It just hurts."

"Did you eat something you shouldn't have? I saw that gigantic box of Milk Duds under your pillow."

Nicole shakes her head. "I didn't eat any this morning."

"Where does it hurt?"

Nicole isn't sure which spot will be the most convincing, but she remembers Ellen Summers had her appendix out last year, and she'd told Nicole her right side hurt like heck. So Nicole puts a hand on her right side. "Here."

Catherine nods and then considers the information. She puts a hand on Nicole's forehead the way their mom does when they're getting sick. "You don't feel hot."

"Do people die if their appendix is bad?"

Catherine's expression becomes a cloud of worry. "Maybe you should go to the nurse's office."

Nicole shakes her head. "No, I don't want to without you. Can't we go on the canoe ride and see how it is when we get back? If I'm with you, you can keep an eye on me."

Catherine glances at Johnny again, and Nicole realizes she doesn't want to miss the canoe ride because that would mean missing out on Johnny. "Okay, but if you get worse while we're out there, we'll have to come back and go to the infirmary."

Nicole nods, remembering to keep her face convincingly concerned, her hand on her side.

The canoes arrive, the college-student counselors pulling them on shore and making sure everyone gets a spot on one. And as they paddle for the center of the lake, a hot July morning sun draping their shoulders, Nicole glances back. Johnny is in the last canoe with Corinne Matthews. By all accounts, he appears to have forgotten about Catherine. And if Nicole feels a smidge of guilt, she tells herself Johnny would never have been good enough for Catherine, anyway.

No boy will ever be good enough for Catherine.

Chapter Sixteen

"You only live once, but if you do it right, once is enough."
— Mae West

Catherine

ANDERS HAS TO work at the spa for the afternoon. Just as well. I park myself on the beach, the pink-toweled chair lulling me into a couple of naps that prove I'm a complete no-hang. I also down a large bottle of Evian and prop up the sign in the sand that brings the waiter over. I order another one and yield to his recommendation of a garden salad that comes with grilled artichokes.

Once he returns with the tray holding my salad and bottled water, I sit up in the chair and pull a novel from my canvas bag, attempting to read while I eat the admittedly delicious lunch.

But my thoughts refuse to stay on the plot, veering instead to last night's moonlit beach and the flashes of memory in which I can still feel Anders' mouth on mine, the hard outline of his body beneath mine.

Heat fans through my belly, and I blink away the memories, telling myself I should know better at my age. I use my fork to toy with another bite of salad, my appetite suddenly dulled under the realization that I am yearning for something I most assuredly am not going to have.

Before coming on this trip, I would have declared myself not even remotely interested in a relationship. Three years, and I haven't been out on a single date. I've wondered if there was something wrong with me. Most women would have gotten over it by now and moved on, or at least that's what the therapist I saw for a year tried to make me see.

But I haven't been ready to move on. I haven't met anyone who made me *want* to move on. Who seemed worth the risk.

Until now?

Is that what I'm thinking about Anders? That he might be worth the risk?

The only reasonable answer to the question is no. He's almost ten years younger than I am. A relationship isn't something that can only last in countable days. Other words might apply. Fling. Hookup. One-night stand.

Is that something I see myself doing?

No.

Casual sex won't fix what's broken inside me.

As tempting as it might be.

Reality check. A gorgeous young man took pity on a woman spending her fortieth birthday alone and asked her out to dinner. Things went a little farther than either of us planned. And here's where reason re-enters the picture.

No more thinking about kissing on the beach. No more wondering what it would be like—

I stop that thought there, place the lid back on my tray and pick up my novel. Vacation. Tanning. Reading. Escape the winter cold for a few sun-kissed days. And then back to reality. Work. And the very different life I lead in New York City.

Chapter Seventeen

"I am always doing that which I cannot do, in order that I may learn how to do it."
— Pablo Picasso

Catherine

OF COURSE MY resolve only lasts until mid-morning the following day when a text from Anders pops up on my phone.

I'd opted out of spin, deciding to run on the beach instead since I didn't have enough faith in my will power to test it by actually having to see him face to face.

The text contains a simple invitation.

Up for an adventure today?

The answer should be simple enough. *Busy with a book on the beach today. No can do.*

But then I tell myself this will end of its own accord. Time will run out like sand in an hourglass, and I'll be on a plane back to Manhattan and the sun, the sand, the sea turtles, and Anders, too, will all be part of the past, sweet memories, and nothing but.

*

ANDERS DRIVES US to Seabird Parasailing in a vintage Land Rover Defender. It's light-blue, boxy with open sides and a canvas roof. The seats are anything but cushy, but it's the perfect island vehicle. I hold my arm out the window, loving the warm air and the unexpected glimpses I get of the ocean along the way.

"There's something I should probably tell you," I say, leaning my head against the seat and trying not to let my concern show.

"You're scared of heights?" he says, nailing me.

"A little?"

"I defer to Eleanor Roosevelt. 'You must do the thing you think you cannot do.'"

"Excellent in theory," I say, glancing out my side of the truck where a trio of goats are grazing the yard of a small house. "What if I get up there and decide I can't do it?"

"I'll be right beside you. They have a two-person parasail."

I admit to breathing a sigh of relief. "If I fall out, does that mean you'll dive in after me?"

He laughs, hanging a left on a road that winds toward the ocean. "At your service, ma'am."

I smile and shake my head, wondering how I let myself get talked into this. "You know my original idea was something benign, like a picnic."

"You'll do great."

"How do you know that?"

"Because you don't like to let things beat you."

I lean out and give him a look. "And how do you know that?"

"I pay attention. I want to know what makes you tick."

Something short and sarcastic rises to the tip of my tongue, but I press my lips together, and turn my head, not at all sure what to make of that assertion. I think of Connor and the last few years of our marriage. Of how I gradually became more and more aware of his lack of interest in me, in who I was as a person. The thought ignites a pain in my chest, and I realize yet again how quickly I can see myself through the lens of a husband no longer in love with his wife.

"Hey." Anders presses his hand on top of mine. "Come back. Be here for now. No before. No after. Just here. Now."

I swing my gaze to his, wondering how it's possible to feel this connection with someone I've known for mere days. How is it possible for him to all but read my mind?

But I want to do exactly what he's just asked me to do. I don't want to see myself as rejected wife, betrayed sister. I want to be a blank canvas. Figure out which colors paint a new me, a me I can see with new eyes.

I catch a glimpse of a parasail on the horizon ahead of us. Anders points, and I nod once. "I can't wait," I say. And I actually mean it.

*

LESS THAN AN hour later, we hang high in

the sky, at least four hundred feet above the slightly choppy deep blue ocean. I don't even know how I managed to hook myself into the harness, sit calmly on the back of the boat as the attendant double-checked to make sure everything was secure. Just as the boat started to move, and the parasail began slowly lifting us into the air, I let out a little scream, and Anders reached over to take my hand, clasping his fingers through mine.

His touch was like a release valve though which all my anxiety just flowed out into nothingness. Now, I am simply here in this moment, suspended in the warm Caribbean sky with a man who's making me see the world from a different point of view.

He leans in now and says, "High enough?"

I nod. "Plenty high."

He raises his voice so I can hear him. "Did you know there's a type of vulture that's been recorded at 37,000 feet? Commercial airliners fly around 35,000."

"How?" I ask. "What about oxygen?"

"They have a kind of hemoglobin that makes them much more efficient at oxygen intake."

"That's impressive, but I'm good right here," I say. I lean back, give him an assessing look. "You know a lot."

He tips his head, shrugs. "I like to read. I've never bought a TV because I don't want to give up my book time at night."

I smile at this. "You really are one surprise after another."

"I'm not sure that's a compliment."

"It is, actually," I say. "It is."

We make our way along the coast, far enough out to avoid snorkelers and fishing boats, but still with an incredible view of the mansions lining the beachfront. I spot the pink chairs and umbrellas of the Sandy Lane beach and marvel again at what a beautiful place it is.

Another few minutes, and the driver swings the boat in a wide arc, and we head back the way we came. Something I've never felt before sweeps over me, and I suddenly have a glimpse of the life I've been living as if I'm looking at it from high above my actual existence. It looks small and questionable, as if its pieces are constructed of toothpicks instead of timbers, capable of toppling at the first strong wind.

Was that the life I meant to build?

I close my eyes for a moment against the undeniable truth. No. I'd meant to do the opposite, actually.

And yet here I am, aware as I have never been before, that I am living a life I am not sure I want to go back to.

Chapter Eighteen

"Sometimes it just feels really really wonderful to be alive."

— Doug Coupland

Catherine

WE LAND ON the parasail boat's platform.

As my feet touch the rubberized surface, I feel as if I've just climbed Mount Everest. "Let's do it again."

Anders laughs. "Thrill junkie. I knew you had it in you."

The young man who helped us out of the harnesses smiles at me and says, "You come back tomorrow. We'll make a time for you."

I smile back at him, saying, "That was one of the most fun things I've ever done."

I'm not sure who looks more pleased, him or Anders. The driver eases the boat back to the beach, and once we're close enough in, Anders and I climb out, thanking him for the ride.

We're headed back to the Jeep when I notice the

sprinkle of rain on my shoulders. I look to the sky, see the dark, almost isolated cloud that is opening its contents above us. Anders grabs my hand, and we run to the Land Rover. He opens my door, and I climb inside, pushing my now wet hair back from my face.

He climbs in the driver's side and with a hand on the steering wheel, looks at me with a half-smile. "We need to make you a list."

"Of what?" I ask, hearing the teasing note in his voice.

"Things you've never done before."

"Oh, a bucket list, you mean?"

"Not a list for preparing to die. You need a list for living. A life list."

"Well, that was a good one to start with," I concede. "Never imagined myself doing that."

He laughs a light laugh, starts the engine. "Show you where I live?"

I see the line I'm about to cross, as if it's been drawn out between us in red paint.

Sensible Catherine would say, "Better get back to the hotel."

Newly adventurous Catherine says, "I'd love to see where you live."

*

BY THE TIME we make the turn onto the drive leading to a lovely, surprisingly large off-white stucco house with a slate roof, the rain has begun to pour in earnest, pelleting the windshield like diamonds being hurled from the sky. Thunder rumbles an ominous soundtrack. Anders cuts the engine, and says, "We can wait here, or make a run for it."

I open my door. "I'm game if you are."

We race to the front entrance where he pulls a key from his pocket and opens the heavy mahogany door.

We're both soaked, my T-shirt and shorts sticking to me.

"I'll just grab some towels," he says, disappearing into a bathroom to the right of the foyer. He returns a few seconds later with two thick white towels, passing one to me and drying off with the other.

I run it across my hair and try to absorb some of the moisture from my shirt. I wrap the towel around my shoulders, taking in the house before us. The foyer is two stories high and opens into a very large living area with wide glass doors that offer a view of the beach and ocean beyond. A well-appointed kitchen sits to the left. I note the Wolf stove with its trademark red knobs. The flooring is a beautiful travertine stone in an antique white.

Canvas paintings add vibrant color to the neutral walls. Casual, dark leather furniture sits on top of a sea-green rug. The house is impressive, yet welcoming. "This is beautiful," I say, not hiding my surprise. "Wall Street must have been very good to you."

He shrugs. "I left some in the market, but I have to admit, as investments go, I'd rather live in one than look at it on paper."

"Real estate good here?"

"I bought this place at a noted market low. If I

needed to sell, I'd come out pretty well. And you know what they say. God isn't making any more land."

"True," I say.

"Can I get you a dry shirt? Don't think I have any shorts that are going to work, but-"

"A dry T-shirt would be great."

"Be right back."

The house is one level, and he jogs off down the hall to our left. I walk over to the glass doors, staring out at the rain that has now lowered its intensity, washing the heat from the cascade of vivid bougainvillea draping the wall between the pool and beach. I wonder what it would be like to live here, and I know a stab of envy that is not typical of me.

"Here you go," he says, returning to hand me a white T-shirt with Sandy Lane Barbados scripted across the front in pink. "A friend of mine left it here after a visit. She's not as small as you, but it should do."

I take it, thanking him, resisting the urge to tease more information out of him regarding the friend.

He has changed his shirt and shorts and is now dry except for his damp hair. "You can change in that bathroom," he says, pointing to the one in the foyer.

I close the door behind me, flicking on the light and studying myself in the mirror above the sink. One thing is for sure. Wet hair is not my friend. I run my hands through it, trying to revive its lift and then decide it's a lost cause. I pull off my wet shirt and replace it with the dry one.

When I return, he's in the kitchen, standing in front of the open fridge. "Beer? Bottled water?"

"Water's good," I say, not yet able to tolerate the idea of alcohol.

He hands me a cold bottle of Evian. I twist off the top and take a sip. "Do you miss anything about your old life?"

"Sometimes. I miss how exciting the city can be. But then I remind myself I live in a place people dream about vacationing in. And too, living there meant doing something I no longer want to do every day."

"Working in a job you hate?"

"I can't say I hated it. But it owned me. I don't want to be owned anymore."

I nod, wishing I didn't understand exactly what he's saying. But I do.

I'm quiet for a few moments, and then, "When you were younger, chasing after all that, did you ever imagine you'd feel that way?"

He laughs a dry laugh. "No." He shakes his head. "No. I wanted to make a life I could call my own. Prove that I could be somebody worth keeping."

A little wave of shock ripples through me at the raw truth exposed in the words. He realizes he's revealed more than he meant to and brightens his expression.

"Whoa. Didn't mean to go there."

I reach out and cover his hand with mine. "I'm sorry those things happened to you."

"It's okay–" he starts, but I stop him again.

"It's not," I say, squeezing his hand, and then

pulling mine away under the increasing intimacy between us.

"I didn't tell you about my childhood to make you feel sorry for me," he says, again attempting lightness. "It was what it was. And I try to believe that we are who we become because of every single thing that happens to us. My goal is to keep heading for a better place."

I glance around us at the wonderfully comfortable home, at the beckoning blue ocean beyond its glass doors. "I think you have certainly done that," I say softly.

The rain has stopped, the clouds lifting as if they know they've exceeded their allotted time, and the sun makes a welcome reappearance. I shake my head a little, and say, "Here, the rain ducks in for a few minutes, and then it's gone again."

"Yeah. Unlike New York where gray needs to be a favorite color, right?"

"The winter is when it gets to me. I'm told I have seasonal affective disorder, so I've had to find ways to lift the winter blahs."

"A change of locale would do it," he says, leaning a shoulder against the door frame and throwing the solution out as if it's an actual possibility.

"As part of the IPO, I agreed to five years as acting CEO. I owe them two more." I hear myself saying this as if it's actually a consideration that I might leave. When had that thought planted itself in my mind?

"Do you intend to stay on after that?" Anders asks quietly.

"I've never really thought about doing anything else. I went to the Savannah College of Art and Design. That's where I had my original ideas about ActivGirl. There were times when I would stay up all night sketching designs. I had no idea how I would get the money to start my own company, but I knew I would someday. I wanted it that much."

"And now?"

"The company isn't really the same since we went public. Being accountable to other people means editing decisions for reasons I might not have before."

"Has that been hard for you?"

I tip my head, concede the truth. "Type A, oldest child, not good at taking advice or orders from others. That's me."

He smiles. "Also the reasons you were able to build the company in the first place."

"Double-edged sword, I guess."

"Most things have one."

"It was so exciting to think we had reached a point where others would want to heavily invest. I went in to work the morning the IPO was to be announced feeling on top of the world. The memory has gotten a little muddied by the fact that it was also the day my marriage fell apart."

He looks a little shocked. "That sucks."

"Is what it is," I offer back.

"You don't have to do that."

"Do what?"

"Act like it's no big deal."

I shrug. "I try not to re-dig the hole on a regular basis."

"Are they together? Your sister and your ex?"

I shake my head.

"Have you and your sister worked things out?"

I look out at the ocean, try to keep my expression neutral. "I can't seem to go there."

"And who could blame you? But maybe you need to. For you."

I hang my gaze on the sun, now fully in charge of its sky again, and wait for the always present wave of bitterness to cascade up from the wound deep inside me. But it doesn't come today. I don't feel anything, actually, except a completely surprising wash of calm. Which brings with it, a single question. What if he's right?

Chapter Nineteen

"How ridiculous and how strange to be surprised at anything which happens in life."
— Marcus Aurelius

Catherine

ANDERS HAS GONE into the kitchen to get us another bottle of water when a knock sounds at the door.

"Probably just a delivery," he calls out. "Would you mind checking?"

"Sure." I walk through the foyer to the door, pulling it open with the full expectation of seeing a guy in a brown uniform holding a package. But that's not what I find. Instead, a beautiful young woman stands at the entrance. I stare at her for a moment, taking in her glossy long, dark hair and green eyes. She's five-ten in flat sandals and short-shorts, her arms and legs lean and toned, her posture that of a runway model.

"Oh," she says, her hand poised in mid-knock again. "Hello."

"Hi," I say.

She peers around me, obviously surprised to find me answering the door. "Is Anders here?"

"Ah, yes, he is," I say, stepping back.

She stops me with, "That's okay. I wanted to surprise him. We haven't seen each other in a while."

"Oh. Sure. And you are?" I can't resist adding that, even as I realize it is none of my business who she is.

"Celeste. Antoine. I pop in whenever I'm on the island for a shoot. Are you staying with-"

I don't let her finish the sentence, "Oh, no. I was just leaving, in fact. If you don't mind, I'll grab your taxi." I wave a hand at the white van that has started to back out of the driveway.

"You don't have to go-" she calls out behind me, but the driver has stopped, and I'm running across the pavement to slide open the side door, climbing in with a quick, "Can you please take me to the Sandy Lane Hotel?"

He looks at me from the rearview with a question in his eyes, but says politely, "Of course. Not a problem."

I glance at the front door where Anders is now standing with the beautiful Celeste, watching me go with a look that gives away nothing of what he is thinking. It is impossible not to notice what a magnificent pair the two of them make, young and absurdly gorgeous. Perfect for each other, in fact.

And as the van winds its way back down the drive

to the main road, I stare out the window, feeling every bit my age. And then some.

*

BACK AT THE hotel, I really don't know what to do with myself.

In my room, I stand before the bathroom mirror, studying my reflection under the undeniable realization that I have been acting like someone I am not, a woman I have never been. Had I really thought there could be something between Anders and me?

Heat splashes up my neck, reddens my face. I force myself to note the color in my cheeks because I am fully aware that I have made a fool of myself. What had I been thinking? Had I been that starved for attention? Suffering from a neglect so intense that I had no problem offering up my dignity in return for the feeling that a man like Anders might be attracted to me?

I drop my head back, let out a long sigh. In this moment, I really hate myself.

Did I do this deliberately? Set myself up for another round of humiliation?

I lift my head, stare down the mirror. *Get real, Catherine.* Life is not a book. Life is not a movie. There really aren't any happy endings. Interludes of things that look like they could go that way, maybe. But if the price to be paid for such temporary self-delusion is another crack in the heart, it's not a price I can afford.

I'm a divorced forty-year-old, on vacation, alone. It's time I started acting like one.

Chapter Twenty

"Honesty is the fastest way to prevent a mistake from turning into a failure."
— James Altucher

Anders

WE'VE BEEN A casual thing, Celeste and I.

We met at a party on a yacht full of Europeans spending a week docked in Barbados. I'd been invited by a couple staying at the hotel for a few days. Celeste had been traveling for a couple of weeks with the owners of the yacht who were old friends of her parents in Paris.

Neither of us was interested in anything other than casual, and by mutual agreement, we spent time together whenever she was in the area. I had never minded the other times she dropped in out of the blue, and I certainly can't be unhappy with her for doing so today. Until now, I've had no reason to mind.

We're standing in the kitchen, making awkward

small talk. She walks over to the fridge, pulls out the half bottle of white wine she'd left unfinished her last visit, grabs a glass from the cabinet and pours it three-quarters full.

With her back to me, she takes a long sip, then turns to face me with a question in her eyes. "Would you rather I go?"

"Celeste, I'm sorry. I-"

"It is okay. I did not tell you I was coming." She lifts her shoulders. "I am understanding of our agreement." She leans against the kitchen counter, crosses her arms and holds the glass high to the right. "We have not asked commitment of one another."

"No," I agree. "We haven't."

"Maybe I should have, hmm?" she asks with a small smile and a flirty look.

We study each other for several drawn out seconds. "I don't really know what's happening with me."

"You are interested in her?"

Even if I answered yes, it wouldn't change the fact that it has no hope of going anywhere. "She's only here on vacation."

"So another me?"

"No," I say, but I'm not sure it's for the reasons she's guessing. Casual isn't what I feel about Catherine.

"She looked hurt," Celeste says quietly. "She has feelings for you?"

"I don't think so."

"I think so."

We hold each other's gaze, and I feel bad because I'm the one who's changed things.

She sets her glass of wine on the counter, walks over and stands in front of me, less than an inch of air separating us. We stand that way for a string of moments, and I can feel her letting my body remember her. She leans in then and brushes my mouth with hers, her eyes closing and then opening, gauging my response.

"You say you don't know what is going on with you where she is concerned. Why don't you let me help you to figure this out?"

When I don't turn away, she kisses me again, this time opening her mouth fully to mine. I feel my reluctance, but admit my own need to decide if anything has changed. Since the moment I set eyes on her, my head has been full of Catherine Camilleri. To a degree even I realize makes no sense.

I loop an arm around Celeste's waist and reel her in.

Chapter Twenty-one

"One must be careful not to take refuge in any delusion."
— James Baldwin

Catherine

IT'S BEEN A full day since I left Anders' house, and I'm at loose ends.

In the twenty-four hours since then, I feel like I've crashed from a sugar high. I've been in the movie, indulging in Coke and Milk Duds in the dark, and now the movie's over, and I've got to walk out into the too-lit lobby and acknowledge my sin.

Vacation without the undercurrent of sexual tension.

It's not like I didn't do it to myself.

Had I really thought there could ever be something physical between us?

The answer is yes. Somewhere, deep down, yes. Had started to yearn for it. Want it in the way of something you know is impossible but let take root inside of you, anyway.

Foolish and forty. That's me.

What I know is that if I'm going to stay here for the rest of my vacation and not head back to Manhattan as the more sensible me would do, then I need to hit rewind and finish out the version of this escape I should have been doing all along.

Having spent the morning at the beach, I decide to go to the pool.

It's a short walk across from the main part of the hotel. The pool connects to the spa, the tile a beautiful deep blue, the water appealingly tempting. There's a swim-up bar, and I see a few people seated on the bar stools ordering drinks.

The pool attendant welcomes me and leads me to a chair which he covers in a thick blue towel. I give him a tip, and he leaves me with a smile. It's nearly four o'clock, the sun still hot in its now clear sky. I decide to take a swim and spend the next twenty minutes paddling from one end to the other, snagging a float and climbing on face down.

"Why, hello!"

I look up to see Madeline from the plane sitting on the step at the edge of the pool. She's wearing a pretty green one-piece, and I have to admire how she has taken care of herself. She's proof that muscles don't have to atrophy, skin doesn't have to wrinkle.

"Hi, Madeline. You look so pretty."

"Why, thank you, dear. I'm hoping this suit doesn't scream 'made for someone much younger'."

I smile and shake my head. "It's perfect. How is your trip so far?"

"Exactly as I had hoped it would be. And yours?"

"It's been wonderful," I say, skimming a hand through the refreshing water.

"Been?"

"Is, I mean."

She gives me a long look, as if she knows I'm leaving something out. "Have you met anyone?"

"Everyone's been really nice," I say, avoiding the question.

She laughs lightly, on to me. "Anyone special?" she persists.

"Out of my league, I'm afraid," I finally admit.

"Who could be out of your league?" she asks, sounding truly surprised.

"Ah, he is," I say, unwavering.

"Why ever?"

"Younger, gorgeous, taken."

"The first two, no. The last? Hm."

"Yeah."

"At least you're putting yourself out there."

"I didn't mean to. It just kind of happened."

"How do you know there's someone else?"

"I met her, actually."

Madeline's expression falls, and I can see she's truly sorry for me.

"It's okay," I say. "Holiday romances only happen in novels and movies."

She raises an eyebrow. "I'm proof that's not true, but I'm sorry yours didn't work out. I have an idea. Why don't we ask if there's availability for a massage? My treat."

"You don't have to do that."

"I want to," she says, standing to step out of the

pool and grab the white robe on a chair behind her. "I'll be right back."

I watch her walk inside the spa, certain she'll have success with the appointments. Madeline approaches life as if it can't possibly tell her no.

And it doesn't. She's back in less than five minutes, smiling. "They can take us in half an hour. Want to make use of the sauna before then?"

"Why not?" I get out of the pool, towel off long enough that I'm not dripping water as we make our way into the inviting spa, stopping at the front desk to confirm our appointments and taking the elevator down to the first floor where we make use of the changing area. The white robe is fluffy and comfortable. We follow the hallway to a door that leads outside to the dry sauna and an outdoor hot tub.

We try the sauna first, and in less than five minutes, Madeline opts for the hot tub. I sit on the wooden bench, not minding the sweat that trickles down the back of my neck. Through the glass front of the sauna, I watch Madeline step into the water and paddle out of sight.

I lean back and close my eyes, startled a few seconds later when the door opens. I look up to see a very tall, very familiar figure stepping inside.

It can't be.

But it is.

She realizes it's me in the same moment I recognize her.

"Oh," she says, and it is clear she's not really happy to see me. "Hello, again."

"Hi," I say, more than a little puzzled to find her

here in the sauna with me instead of back at Anders' house. And in his bed.

"This is awkward," she says, taking a seat on the far side of the bench.

"Sorry," I say, standing to leave.

"No, no," she says, waving me back onto the seat. "We are both adults."

Me more so than you, I want to say, but don't.

"I'm not exactly used to rejection," she offers in a low voice.

I give her a full look, noting the clear hurt on her face. I have no idea what to say. "Rejection?" I manage.

"Not my normal experience with men."

We're silent for several long seconds, and then she adds, "You are in his head."

To say the words shock me would be an understatement. "I don't think you're right about that."

She laughs softly. "Oh, I'm right. Believe me."

She drops her towel, fully naked under a sheen of sweat. I'm still wearing my robe, and even though I'm at the point of my skin igniting, I'm not about to take it off and suffer the comparison.

"Is this a casual thing for you?"

"Ah, it's not a thing. We haven't-"

"You certainly have something to look forward to then. Anders is-" She breaks off and finally adds, "Difficult to live up to."

I'm pretty sure I know what she means by this. "Are you in love with him?"

"I could be," she answers honestly. "If he would give me the go ahead."

"Go ahead?"

"Some indication he could love me back."

"Oh."

I hear the longing in her voice, and oddly enough, I feel sorry for her. In the past twenty-four hours, I've done my share of mooning over Anders, and I'm sure she has real history to mourn. I only had the fantasy of it.

"I shouldn't be a reason for you two not to-" I break off there, not sure how to finish.

"Yeah, well, when one's not into it, kind of not the same."

"I find it hard to believe any man would kick you out of bed."

She shrugs. "Anders is different. There's got to be a connection there. I thought we had one, but apparently you've made him see it differently."

A young woman dressed in a spa uniform appears at the door, opens it to say, "Ms. Camilleri?"

"Yes," I answer.

"The masseuse is ready for you."

"Oh. Thank you." I stand, sweat dripping down my face and neck to be absorbed by the robe. "I'm sorry for the disappointment, Celeste."

She makes an attempt at a cheery smile. "Just don't let it be for nothing. Anders says your heart has been broken," she says. "He is worth the risk."

*

MADELINE HAS ALREADY gone in for her massage, and I follow the young lady who had come to get me down the marble floor hall with its wall sconce lighting to a room where she knocks once and opens the door for me.

The masseuse is waiting inside, a woman with kind eyes and hands that prove to be up to the job of dissolving the knots of tension in my shoulders and back.

"Ooh," she says. "You have not been doing enough relaxing. More time on the beach, less time in your head."

She uses the bottom of her hand to knead a particularly resistant knot. I moan under the pain-pleasure of it, trying not to let my thoughts wander to the very unsettling conversation I'd just had with Celeste.

Which is impossible.

Don't let it be for nothing.

Had he really turned her down?

And could it really be because I'm in his head? *Me?*

"Blank mind," the masseuse orders. "At least let me get rid of the knots before you start putting them back again."

I squeeze my eyes shut, force my thoughts to something neutral, something that doesn't inspire tension. Easier said than done.

Chapter Twenty-two

"There is no point in using the word 'impossible' to describe something that has clearly happened."
— Douglas Adams

Anders

I'VE BEEN BETTING myself she won't show up for class again this morning.

When I see her walk in the door, my stomach takes a nose-dive, and I have to wonder what the heck is going on with me. First, ending things with Celeste. And now I'm acting like a teenager waiting to find out if the first girl I've ever liked likes me back.

She avoids eye contact, taking a bike in the back. I walk around the room, helping the other riders adjust their seat height, pull the handlebars closer, anything to avoid looking at Catherine.

I glance at my watch. It's time to start. I lower the lights in the room. I walk to the front, climb on my bike and hit the iPad beside me to start the music. It's a full class this morning, and I'm glad because I have a variety of places to rest my gaze other than on Catherine. Even so, I'm able to take in her movements from the corner of my vision, and I'm noting the nice color to her arms and legs beneath the short black shorts. Gone is the New York winter pallor, a healthy sun-kissed glow in its place. Her blonde hair is snagged in a high ponytail, dancing off her shoulders as she pulls a towel and bottle of water from her bag, stowing it at the back of the bike, and then adjusting the seat to the proper height, all without looking at me, or giving any indication she knows I'm in the room.

So I play it cool too. I crank the music, climb on the bike and start pedaling while jumping into the instructor mode my classes like best. Coach with a sense of humor, prodding them to join me in meeting the goals of the class.

Ten minutes in, everyone is sweating which tells me I'm doing my job. I'm thirty minutes into the class before I let myself meet Catherine's gaze head on. Neither of us looks away for a full five seconds, and I don't bother to hide the heat in my eyes. I intend for her to look away first, and she does, dropping her head and increasing her pedal speed, as if she can outrun this thing between us.

But she can't.

And I don't intend to let her.

*

THE ROOM EMPTIES out pretty quickly. There is the buffet waiting, after all. Catherine is about to make her getaway through the open door when I call her name.

She stops, stands stiffly, and then slowly turns to face me. She says nothing, simply meeting my gaze and holding it as if she is forcing herself not to glance away this time.

"Can we talk?" I ask.

"About?"

"Yesterday."

"There's nothing you need to explain, Anders."

"I'm pretty sure there is."

"I saw Celeste at the spa last night."

I take this in, nod once. "So you know we didn't-"

"It's none of my business," she says, repositioning her bag on her shoulder.

"What if I said I'd like it to be?"

"Anders."

Just the way she says my name reveals exactly what she's thinking. We're a waste of time. She lives in New York City. I live here. She'll be gone in a matter of days. I'm not going anywhere. "I know," I say. "And if you go strictly with logic, you're exactly right. Only where you're concerned, I'm not feeling very logical."

She wants to argue. I see it on her face. She bites her lip once, sighs as if giving in to something she doesn't understand. And then she says, "Would you like to join me for breakfast?"

*

WE SIT AT a table close to the beach. An umbrella protects us from the already heated sun, and all around us birds sing happy songs, the lyrics of which I suspect have something to do with bountiful food and life in paradise.

The waitress approaches our table with a smile and asks for the room number. Catherine tells her and then adds, "I'll have a guest on my ticket this morning."

"Not a problem," the pretty young woman says, looking at me with a smile.

"Thanks," I say.

As soon as she leaves the table, Catherine pushes back her chair and says, "Come on. You need to see why your students struggle to sweat so much in your class."

I follow her to the area where the buffet is set up. We make our way to the juice bar first, and I take in the individual signs identifying what is in each pitcher. "Carrot, green juice, watermelon," I say. "This looks like it won't do too much damage."

She smiles and says, "Oh, you haven't been challenged yet."

We take our juice back to the table and then reach for plates at the omelet bar. We meander in the direction of our individual choices, until I'm finally heading back to the table with enough calories to get me through at least seventy-two hours.

Catherine is already seated, and she takes in my heaping plate with a knowing smile. "See what I mean," she says.

"Yeah, I think I do. What is it about a buffet that turns innocent men into gluttons?"

She laughs softly. "Women too," she says, pointing at her own plate.

"I should have stuck with the juice," I say.

For the first couple of minutes, we eat in silence, and I finally put down my fork and look at her. "Everything you've thought about why we would be wrong to continue this thing we've been flirting with between us is almost for sure correct. We live thousands of miles apart, have chosen completely different lifestyles. In a few days, you'll be gone. I'll still be here."

She puts down her fork, watching me with conflicted eyes. "Yes. And yet."

"And yet," I repeat.

"I don't want to close the door."

"Neither do I."

"If we can agree that we know what this is, something that has no hope of living beyond my time here. . ."

I wait as she lets the words trail off. I take a sip of my juice, set the glass down and nod once. We're both adults living in reality. If anyone understands what reality is, I do. "Agreed," I say.

Chapter Twenty-three

"Loneliness and the feeling of being unwanted is the most terrible poverty."
— Mother Teresa

Nicole

SHE VOLUNTEERS AT the no-kill shelter in West Palm Beach two or three mornings each week. When she first decided to volunteer at the animal shelter, she knew she had to go to the one where the dogs and cats were assured of getting out by adoption. She couldn't volunteer at the one where they have a certain number of days to be found by their forever family or receive an orange tag on their door that tells the euthanasia tech who will be put to sleep at the end of the day.

Nicole knows this because she used to volunteer at the public shelter in a county outside Greenville, South Carolina the summer after her senior year in high school. Catherine was already in college and had won a scholarship to spend the summer at a design school in Italy, and Nicole had been incredibly lonely. She'd thought spending hours working at the shelter with dogs and cats would be a great way to involve herself in something good and combat her loneliness with animals because she loved being around them.

Nothing would have been further from the truth.

On her first day at the South Carolina shelter, she went through the necessary volunteer orientation with one of the full-time shelter employees. He was a gruff older man who had been there for years according to another volunteer, and he never smiled when he looked at the dogs or cats. The first warning sign for Nicole should have been his advice "not to get attached." She'd assumed he meant because they would be adopted, and it would be painful to see them leave with their new family. She understood that, but it seemed to her that she would be happy to see them leaving with someone who would love them.

For the first week, she was only allowed to work at the front desk. She wasn't allowed to go into the kennels, and although she saw dogs and cats when owners brought them in to sign them over to the shelter, she did not see them again once they were taken back. One day, she asked the shelter manager when she would be able to work in the back. The manager was a woman in her forties who also didn't smile very much and looked at Nicole as if she had grave doubts about her ability to do much more than hand people relinquishment documents and answer the telephone.

"I'm not sure you'll be suited to working in the back. Let's keep you out front for now."

Nicole wanted to argue with her, but she wasn't exactly sure what the basis of her argument should be because she didn't know why the woman thought she wouldn't be suited. And so she did her best to shine in the position she'd been put in, greeting people with smiles even when she began to wonder how so many owners could drive their pet to the shelter and hand them over to her at the front desk as if they were a piece of mail that had been delivered by mistake.

She began to wonder if the people had any idea how scared their dog was when he or she realized their person had left them, how they barked or meowed to be allowed to follow them out the door. She wondered if they felt any guilt at all for raising a puppy to love them and their children and then "getting rid" of them because they chewed the corner of the living room rug when they'd left them home all day alone.

As the weeks went on, Nicole's smiles were less ready, and her stomach hurt when the front door opened, and in walked another person with a dog so old he couldn't clearly see where he was being taken, a dog who had devoted his life to loving his person and should be allowed to die at home in the place he knew and loved. She wondered how anyone could do such a thing.

It was on a Saturday morning that a man in a baseball cap walked in to the shelter with just such a dog. The man couldn't look her in the eye when she handed him the relinquishment form. He was well-dressed and spoke like a person with a good amount of education. Out the front window of the shelter, she could see that he had pulled up in a Lexus sedan. The dog was black with a gray muzzle, and he had trouble standing on the tile floor. His back legs shook, and he finally lay down beside the man's feet, his head raised as if he didn't want to let the man out of his sight.

Nicole's heart throbbed, and she tried not to look at the dog for the duration of the man's filling out the form. She saw the number 16 filled in beside Age. She wasn't allowed to question him or do anything at all except take the form when he was done. When he signed his name at the bottom, he held the dog's leash up and waited for her to walk around the desk to take it from him.

The man turned to walk away. The dog tried to stand to follow him, but his hind legs slid on the tile, and he fell onto his stomach.

"What's his name?" Nicole called after the man.

The man stopped at the door, still not letting himself look at the dog. "Nash," he said.

The dog's tail began to thump, but the man opened the door and walked out.

The dog again tried to stand up, whimpering now. Nicole dropped to her knees and scooped him up, walking over to a nearby chair and sitting down with him on her lap.

"It's okay," she said in a soft voice. "I'm sorry. I'm so sorry. You're going to be okay though."

Nash shook, so hard that she could hear his teeth

chattering. She held him closer and rubbed his head. He tucked his nose inside her armpit, as if he couldn't bear to look at his surroundings or face what was happening to him.

The door to the shelter area opened, and Jerry, the morning's attendant walked out. He saw Nicole holding the dog and said, "Owner surrender?"

She nodded, not trusting herself to speak.

"I'll take it back."

Nicole wanted to protest, to keep the dog here with her a little longer, at least until he stopped shaking, but Jerry reached for him and was walking for the door before she could say a word. There was no one else out front then, and Nicole could no longer hold back her sobs. She felt Nash's terror and sadness as if it had been injected into her own bloodstream, and she sat there absorbing it on a level she had never imagined possible.

And she knew with a sudden, undeniable conviction that she had to take Nash home with her. She ran to the front desk, dialed the number to her house and prayed her mom would answer. Her dad was playing golf this Saturday morning, and her mom had planned to run some errands. The phone rang and rang with no answer. She glanced at the clock on the wall. Eleven-forty five. The shelter would close in fifteen minutes.

She tried her mom again, still with no answer. At five minutes until twelve, she decided she would adopt Nash and take him home without asking her parents. She knew they would understand once she had explained the situation.

No one else had come in to the shelter so she decided to go back and tell the attendant she was going to adopt Nash. She stepped through the door that led to the kennel area, and the first thing she noticed was the silence. She walked down the row of cages, frowning when she saw there were no dogs in them. But by the door at the end of the hall, six or eight or ten black bags were stacked alongside each other in a row. Nicole shook her head, trying to process what she was seeing. She realized with a sickening thud of her stomach they were body bags.

"Oh, no," she said out loud. "Nash. Nash!"

She began to scream his name over and over again, running down the hall in the opposite direction to find someone, anyone who could tell her where he was. She stopped outright at the sight of the door at the end of this corridor. A red sign – DO NOT ENTER – hung in the center.

Nicole's mind raced, her thoughts all running into one another at the same rate as her pulse.

The door opened, and Jerry stepped out. She ran to the door. "Where is Nash?"

Jerry looked irritated and said, "You're not supposed to be back here."

"Where is he?!!?" she screamed.

Jerry tried to close the door, but she jerked it toward her, and it opened wide enough for her to see Nash, the sweet old dog she'd promised would be okay, the dog she was going to adopt, lying on the floor on his side, his eyes open wide but now unseeing.

"What did you do?" She sobbed the words at Jerry who jerked the door from her and closed it.

"Owner surrender. We can euthanize those before the owner pulls out of the parking lot. It's Saturday. We empty the kennels for the weekend for whoever hasn't been adopted. What? Don't tell me you didn't know?"

Nicole stumbled backwards, her shoulder crashing into the wall. "No. I. . .I didn't know. How could you? You're a monster!"

"If you're gong to work here, I'd suggest you stay up front where you belong. Behind the desk in Pollyannaville."

Pure hatred filled her, and Nicole turned and ran to her Toyota Corolla in the parking lot. She drove home crying so hard she could barely see through her tears.

Looking back, Nicole knew that this moment, this scene, her own heartbroken sobs marked the beginning of a lifelong depression and sadness that would take root inside her and forever mark the world as a place where horrible things happen. Because despite the fact that the sun shines, that people laugh, that babies are born, horrible, truly horrible and unjust things happen. Every. Single. Day.

*

ON THIS SUNNY, blue day in Florida, Nicole sits in the well-kept yard of the Ruth Ann Cosby No-Kill shelter with an older dog named Callie. They are sitting on the grass, Callie's chin resting on Nicole's knee as she dozes with her eyes closed in the warm sun. Nicole strokes her head, her touch soft and comforting. She isn't sure whether the comfort is for her or the older dog, but the nice thing is that she knows they both have something to give the other.

It's always been like that for her with animals though. She's always felt an acceptance, a connection from them that she has never felt with people. It's as if animals see that part of her she never lets others see, the part that wants to be loved for who she is. She knows that is how she sees them.

She tries not to think about the fact that Callie's family gave her up because she now has trouble making it outside to potty. The shelter vet put her on a medication that has helped her a lot. The family was notified of this, but they did not want to take her back.

Nicole runs her hand across Callie's soft back and wishes for a moment that she could think of her own life with Callie in it. But every time she tries to do that, her thoughts stop at the black wall, and her chest feels as if an enormous block of concrete has been lowered onto it.

Pain floods through her head and rushes through her veins with such force she has to close her eyes against it. She wishes with every good thing left inside her that she could be this little dog's miracle. The undeniable truth though is that she is as far from miracle-material as it is possible to get. Maybe a good family will come for Callie, a family deserving of the love of a good dog like her.

Nicole is not that person, not for Callie, not even for her own parents and sister.

Chapter Twenty-four

"The poetry of the earth is never dead."
— John Keats

Catherine

"YOU'RE REALLY NOT going to tell me where we're going?"

"This is a surprise you'll like. I promise."

It's just before five o'clock in the afternoon, and the sun has started to dip in the pink-streaked sky. The windows are open on the Defender, and the wind, warm and humid, blows my hair back from my face.

I'd like to argue, but honestly, it's easier not to. I settle back in the leather seat and turn my gaze to the island views flowing by, and I'm overcome with a feeling of contentment. When was the last time I felt happy to hand the decision-making over to someone else? Made the choice to be patient and wait for whatever unfolds ahead of me?

Never would be the answer.

But today, I am. I don't understand it. But I am.

We drive for fifteen or twenty minutes more before we turn onto an unpaved road that winds through some palm trees and big, colorful bushes before the ocean appears in front of us. Other cars are parked in the grass at the edge of the sandy beach. A group of people stands to our right. A couple of them glance around and raise a hand when they spot Anders.

I turn a questioning gaze to him. He smiles and relents. "I think I told you I help out with the Sea Turtle project when I'm needed. A bunch of babies hatched out today on Needham's Point Beach, and volunteers have been collecting them to release this evening when they have a better chance of survival."

I draw in a short breath of surprise and delight. "And we get to watch them?"

He laughs, pleased by my response. "Yep. Come on," he says, opening his door and vaulting out of the truck.

I climb out as well. Anders takes my hand and leads me toward the group of a dozen or so people already standing on the beach. I'm surprised, but don't pull away, following him with the same kind of feeling I had as a child on Christmas morning when my sister and I would sneak down early to see what Santa had left under the tree. The thought of Nicole drops an instant veil of sadness over me, but I blink it away, determined to be in this moment, this place. And nowhere but here.

"Hello!"

The woman who calls out to Anders is tall with beautiful dark hair divided into two long braids that hang to her waist. The look on her face is one of happy anticipation. "So glad you could come," she says, and then looking at me, "And you've brought a friend. Welcome."

"Catherine, this is Hannah Brathwaite. She's one of the main reasons here in Barbados that sea turtles have a chance to survive."

I stick out my hand, find her grip warm and firm. "It's so nice to meet you," I say. "What an amazing thing to be a part of."

"It is," she says. "I'm the mad woman rushing beach to beach trying to collect every hatchling possible and release them at the time of day they're most likely to survive."

"Thank you," I say. "For what you do. It's incredible."

Hannah shrugs, smiling. "The reward is all mine. Barbados is fortunate enough to be the nesting home for Hawksbill, Leatherback and Green Turtles. I've always believed that places a heavy responsibility on us as a country to do what we can to protect them."

"Some people wouldn't see it that way."

She shrugs as if she knows this is true. "Leatherback turtles keep fish populations healthy by controlling the number of jellyfish. If they didn't do that, populations of fish larvae would be decimated. They're incredibly important to the ecosystem. The Hawksbill turtles eat sea sponges and help keep them from over-growing on the coral reefs." She lets out a deep breath and smiles. "Okay. Me. Off my soapbox."

"No," I say. "It's fascinating. Really."

"Are you a new citizen to Barbados, Catherine?" she asks, politely curious.

"Ah, no. Just here on vacation," I say, noting the smiling glance she throws Anders, as if I'm not the first vacation romance she's met of his.

It's not as if I should be surprised. He works in a place where he constantly meets new people, and what single woman wouldn't be drawn to him if he gave her that look of interest I am now admittedly familiar with?

"Well," Hannah says, clapping her hands together. "We have ninety-seven babies to release, so we better get busy. It's really nice to meet you, Catherine."

"You too, Hannah."

Once she walks away, Anders touches a hand to my arm and says, "I know what you're thinking."

"I have no right to be thinking anything other than that I'm happy you brought me here."

He gives me a look of surprise, and I watch the desire to question what I've said melt from his face, and he says, "Most of these babies hatched out earlier today."

"It's so nice to see how important they are to the people here." I say, studying the happy faces of the people lined along the beach, waiting for the release.

"This is the time of day when they have the fewest predators. The goal is to give them the greatest chance of survival. Once they're in the ocean, they'll swim up to seventy-two hours, trying to get their bearings and figure out what they're supposed to be doing."

"That's incredible," I say, unable to imagine something so little working that hard.

"Okay, everyone, it's time!" Hannah calls out from the back of the crowd, making her way through with what looks like a wide white tray. Four other volunteers walk behind her carrying similar trays. They move to the center of the crowd, and she says, "If you all could form a line on either side of us, we'll leave the center open for these little guys to have room to do their thing."

It's then that I see inside the trays and spot the dozens of baby turtles scrambling about. They're about the size of a silver dollar with little legs that stick out and are already trying to make a swimming motion. My heart leaps to my throat, and I let out a gasp of delight. "Oh, my gosh, they're adorable."

Anders looks at me and smiles, and I can tell he is pleased that I'm so taken with them.

"We've been collecting this group of hatchlings throughout the day," Hannah explains. "It's a bit of a tedious process because once they're out of the egg, they're ready to go. We hold them in a setting that allows them to remain as rested as possible. If they're put in water to wait for the release, they'll often swim the entire time and be exhausted by the time we're ready to let them go."

Each of the volunteers lines up alongside Hannah and her hatchlings. They squat down and place the trays on the sand. "Our goal is to handle them as little as possible, but we'll take four volunteers to help place them in the sand."

I'm itching to raise my hand, but feel as though

I shouldn't since many of these people are probably locals and much more entitled to the privilege than I am.

Hannah points to the back of the line, calls out a name, another, and another, and then turns toward me. "Catherine, would you like to help?"

I'm stunned into silence, and a wave of happiness sweeps over me, and I'm smiling like I'm in first grade, and the teacher has asked me to be her special helper. I nod and say, "Thank you. I would love to."

I look at Anders. He smiles and says, "Go for it."

Hannah waves me over to her tray, and I drop down on my knees beside her. She glances at me and says, "The look in your eyes reminds me of how I felt when I first heard about the plight of the sea turtles. You're moved by them, aren't you?"

I nod. "Yes. I am."

She smiles at me, and says, "Okay, little guys, welcome to the world."

She picks the first one up and sets it gently on the sand. "Go ahead, Catherine."

I reach for one and set it down beside the other. The volunteers begin placing theirs on the sand, and all of a sudden, the hatchlings start forward, going as fast as their little legs will carry them, straight for the ocean in front of them. We continue placing the other hatchlings on the sand until the trays are empty, and what's before us looks like a crowded highway of tiny turtle cars speeding for the water. I sit back on my heels, taking in the miracle before us.

Hannah glances at me, and a sudden sadness crosses her face like a stray cloud over a blazing sun.

In a low, soft voice, she says, "The odds are so against them. One in one thousand survive to reproductive adulthood."

The words shock me, and I stare at her in disbelief. I turn my gaze to the baby turtles, struggling across the sand with a determination that makes my heart ache in my chest. Their desire to get where they know they're supposed to be and the urgency in their efforts that says they know they must hurry makes me realize how for granted I have taken my own life and all that I have.

And all of a sudden, tears well in my eyes, streaming down my face in a rush of emotion so overwhelming I don't bother to wipe them away. I want to feel this experience. For the past three years, I've been trying not to feel anything, putting my focus on the tasks of my day and plodding through. Not exactly running from life but idling in neutral.

Seeing how badly these little creatures want to live, find what they need to survive, I'm hit with a sudden desire to find my life again, to run toward it with everything that has made me who I am. Standing here on this beach in a place I am beginning to love, I realize I've been considering my life over. Something to be ridden out, all the best parts in the past.

Anders walks forward, puts his hand on my elbow. He smiles as the first of the hatchlings find the water. We both watch as a small wave lifts them up, plants them firmly back on the sand. But they are not to be deterred. They struggle forward once more, so visibly convinced that they know where they belong. The voice inside them is that strong, that innate.

Anders' arm slips around my shoulders. He pulls me in against him, and I hear the voice inside me. Is it really saying what I think it is saying? But there is no doubt. By any reasonable measure, I haven't known him long enough, don't have a log of days, weeks and months spent learning who he is. But my pull to him is as strong as the pull of the ocean to these magnificent little turtles. Just as real. Just as undeniable.

I lean my head against his chest, and I know he feels my acknowledgment in this single gesture. No words needed.

Chapter Twenty-five

"It is only with the heart that one can see rightly; what is essential is invisible to the eye."
— Antoine de Saint-Exupery

Catherine

IT'S DARK BY the time we reach Anders' house.

He's suggested we could make dinner there, and all I know is that I want to be with him, wherever that might be. I can't even explain to myself exactly what I'm feeling. It's almost as if a different person has taken over my mind and body. I have a hunger to experience things all but forgotten as a part of who I am. I used to be adventurous, curious about life and experiences.

Somewhere along the way, I started to believe life didn't have much left to show me. How could I have thought I'd seen all there was to see? How could I have convinced myself that the end of my marriage was the end of me, the end of living my life?

I don't really know how, but I convinced myself of that.

And now? Now, I feel ravenous for more. I feel like a person starved of vital nutrients, as if Anders has slipped a few in my drink, and my body is screaming for more.

We're standing in the kitchen when this realization settles over me, and I am filled with the desire to thank him. But I think it will sound a little crazy if I put it into words, so I say, "Why don't I cook dinner for you? It's the least I can do given what you just showed me."

"You cook?"

"I do."

"I can probably scrounge up some pasta. I have basil growing on the terrace."

"I happen to make a very mean pesto sauce."

He claps his hands together. "All right then. Pasta's in the cabinet there. I'll go pick the basil."

My gaze hangs on his wide shoulders until he disappears through the doors leading outside. I open cabinets until I find the box containing the pasta noodles. It's a good one. Harry Cipriani. If Anders has garlic and olive oil, I'm in business.

I find the oil, also a nice Italian one. I grab a shaker of pink sea salt while I'm at it. In the refrigerator, I spot a glass jar of minced garlic. A blender occupies a corner of the countertop. I've made the pesto so many times, the recipe is committed to memory. I find measuring spoons and scoop out the garlic and drop it into the blender. I add the olive oil, a half cup or so. I then add the salt.

I search around until I locate a large pot, set it in the sink and fill it halfway with water. I then put it on the stove and turn on the heat.

Anders appears with the basil. Its aroma arrives before he does, and I remember how much I love the smell of it fresh from the garden. "My mom used to grow basil in pots in the summer," I say. "It smells so good."

"It does," he agrees. "I love herbs. I keep them growing and use them for cooking and salads. They're highly nutritious. I count them among the nine vegetables I try to eat every day."

"Nine, huh? That's a lot of vegetables."

"It is. I used to hate eating vegetables."

"What changed your mind?" I ask, rinsing the basil under the sink faucet.

He considers my question to the point that I am curious.

When he finally answers, his voice is almost too deliberately casual. "I decided one day I had to figure out what a body needs to stay healthy. I read this book by Dr. Terry Wahls. She basically cured herself of MS by completely changing the way she ate. Nine cups of vegetables per day."

"Wow."

"It sounds like a lot. I'm used to it now. I juice pretty much every morning. That makes a big dent in my daily quota."

"What do you juice?"

"You name it. Carrots. Broccoli. Kale. Celery. Apples. Oranges. Dandelion greens."

"Hard core," I say, smiling.

He laughs a soft laugh. "I guess so." He sobers a little. "I've come to understand the power of food to give our bodies the ability to fight off things we don't want. I didn't used to eat like this though."

Something in the admission makes me want to ask more because there seems to be more beneath the surface I'm missing. I shrug it off and say, "I could be a lot better about what I eat. I actually love salads. I get lazy at night after work and usually opt for something easier."

"I've come up with some shortcuts that make it a little easier."

"Such as?" I drop the basil into the blender, add a half teaspoon of the sea salt.

"I chop vegetables, a lot at once, and store them in a big glass bowl in the fridge. For a single meal, I can take out whatever I want, make a good dressing with my herbs and some olive oil, and I'm set."

"I'm impressed," I say. "I need to do better. In fact, I will do better."

He laughs. "Would you like a glass of wine? I've got a good red."

"I would love one," I say. While he's opening the bottle, I turn on the blender and pureé my ingredients into a pesto that smells like an Italian restaurant when I remove the lid.

Anders leans in and inhales. "That smells incredible. You weren't kidding about the cooking skills."

"You haven't sampled the final product yet," I say. "You might want to hold up on the praise."

He hands me a glass of wine, and I take a sip. "Um. Very good."

"A Chateauneuf du Pape. One of my favorites."

"Love it. Several years ago, I attended a trade show in Paris. I decided to take a few days to explore some of the French countryside and ended up touring a couple of vineyards in this region. It means the Pope's new castle."

"That's cool. Did a pope live there at one time?"

"In the thirteen hundreds, the current pope relocated to Avignon and loved the Burgundy wines and helped them to become much more widely known. Before that, they had been mostly drunk by locals."

He nods and looks at me as if he's seeing me for the first time.

"Ah, sorry. Probably more than you wanted to know about this wine. I'm kind of a geek about knowing the story behind things I like."

"Actually, I like that you're a geek about the things you like."

We stand there in the middle of his kitchen, and I'm overcome with a desire to know him better, to answer my own questions about the life he has made for himself here.

He turns away, sets his glass on the counter and retrieves a spoon to stir the pasta, his back to me. And somehow, I know that he has felt my questions. And all but said the words. Please don't ask.

Chapter Twenty-six

"If you are in a beautiful place where you can enjoy sunrise and sunset, then you are living like a lord."
– Nathan Phillips

Anders

ONCE YOU'VE ACCEPTED the inevitability of death, I mean the inevitability of your own death, living becomes a tricky thing.

When the doctors at Sanoviv finally declared my body cancer-free over two years ago, I had no idea how to navigate the road back to living without the fear that any day could be my last. Death had defined my life long enough that I didn't know how to expect more.

Of course, it could be the last day for any of us, at any time. There's nothing to say that my heart won't stop beating in the middle of the night. That I won't step off a curb in front of a moving bus. I do believe that when it's my time, it's my time. But apparently, it isn't yet. And I wonder on a regular basis if some part of me is afraid to live like I have forever, if that might in some way tempt fate and make it change its mind on the u-turn it gave me after I went to Sanoviv.

I've just stepped back into the house to turn the speakers on outside. I stand now inside the French doors, watching Catherine sit at the edge of the pool, her feet dangling in the water. Her silhouette against the dim lighting around the pool is beautiful, her long blonde hair a curtain against her back. She dips a hand into the surface of the water, lifting it high and letting it trail through her fingers. She does this over and over again, the simple motion cathartic to watch. The moon is large and yellow-orange tonight, and it casts a perfect arc of light across her figure. Staring at her, I am lit with a flame of desire like nothing I have felt in a very long time. With my illness, all physical desire dissolved inside me, and I had no reason to believe it would ever return.

It did when I met Celeste, but it was always marked by reserve, fear, I guess. And so I held some piece of myself back, as if I were living as an imposter, the old me gone forever.

Catherine turns, sees me, holds out her hand. I am torn between a want so strong it is as if it has wrapped its roots around my heart and a terror equally capable of robbing me of all courage to give this thing between us a chance.

I step outside, close the door behind me, walk across the travertine and sit down next to her. The water in the pool glistens beneath the moonlight.

"Hey," she says.

"Hey."

She studies me for several long seconds, and says, "I can go back to the hotel now if you'd like for me to."

Something strong and innate tells me I would be wise to agree that it's time for that. But what I know more than anything right now is that I don't want her to. I want her to stay. "A stronger man would make that happen."

"You are a strong man."

"Not when it comes to you," I admit in a barely audible admission.

She lets out a soft breath, as if she has been holding it, waiting for my answer. She puts her hand over mine, presses her palm against my skin. "There's something you're not telling me," she says. "I can feel it."

Now is the time to confess my history, the truth about my life here. I want to tell her. I need to tell her, but I don't know how to do so in a way that won't cause her to get up and run, as any logical person would do.

"Are you married?" The three word question pops out of her as if she has wanted to ask for some time, but wouldn't allow herself to do so.

The irony does not escape me. My quiet laugh startles her. I shake my head. "No, Catherine. I'm not married."

Relief dances across her expression, as if this is the greatest thing she fears, the worst thing she could think of as a reason not to be with me. And given her history, maybe it would be. But the real reason is far worse.

She runs her hand up my arm, leans in closer, her mouth scant inches from mine. "Oh. Okay. That is really good to hear."

The words whisper across my lips, igniting a fresh heat inside me, the heat of desire, of need, of the kind of want I haven't known for a very long time. Want based on a connection I've never imagined actually finding.

The beat of the music lifts my heartbeat so I feel it against the wall of my chest. I could ruin all of this with a few select words, blow it right out of the realm of possibility. Should I? Am I wrong not to?

She leans in and presses her lips against mine. Her touch is soft, feather-light, but it instantly erases all thoughts from my mind except the need to have her closer. I slip my arms around her waist and lift her onto my lap. She slides a leg on either side of me, wrapping her arms around my neck and kissing me now full on, her mouth letting me know I am welcome, that she wants me in the way every man wants to be wanted. With complete abandon and reckless need.

I take the lead now, kissing her full and long, pressing her back into the palms of my hands. I can feel her breasts through the thin material of my shirt, and all I know is that I want her against me, skin to skin, no barriers between us. She tightens her arms around my neck, opening her mouth to deepen the kiss. She leans back, pulling me into her, and all of a sudden, we are falling backwards, into the pool. I'm on top of her, the weight of my body pushing her deep into the water.

I panic now, reaching for her, pulling her up against me and kicking my way to the surface. When we break through, she immediately starts laughing. Relief floods through me. “I thought I’d drowned you,” I say instantly, anchoring an elbow against the wall of the pool and holding onto her.

She’s still laughing when she wraps her legs around my waist, and her arms are around my neck again, her breasts pressed to my chest. “I think we have a problem,” she says softly.

“Oh, yeah? What’s that?” Desire threads my voice, but I don’t see any point in trying to hide it now.

“I need to get you out of these wet clothes,” she says, starting to unbutton my shirt. “I wouldn’t want you to catch a cold. I mean, just think. You wouldn’t be able to teach spin. And you’d have all those disappointed ladies to contend with.”

“I certainly don’t like disappointing the ladies.”

By now, she’s reached the bottom button. She grazes the back of her hand against my skin, raking it up my abdomen while her gaze drinks me in. “How long did it take you to get that six-pack?”

“A while,” I admit.

“You’re a walking advertisement for your class.”

“You think?”

“I know.”

She slides the shirt from my shoulders and struggles for a moment to get my arms out. Once she wins the battle, she drops it on the tile floor of the pool.

"If you think that's necessary for me," I say, my gaze on her face, "I'd better get yours off too. A cold would ruin the rest of your vacation."

"It would," she agrees softly. "That would be a shame. Staying in my room eating soup with the sun shining outside."

I smile at this and put my attention on the fact that she's wearing some kind of fitted, sleeveless sweater, through which I can clearly see the outline of her lacy bra. I put a hand to the bottom of the sweater, raise one side, then the other. She lifts her arms straight up in assistance and takes it from me.

"Catherine," I say, her name a hoarse plea in my throat. I can't take my eyes off her.

She reaches one hand around to the back of her bra, unhooks it and sends it off into the night.

I swallow once. Hard. "You are so. Incredibly. Beautiful."

She slides her arms around me again, and hides herself against my chest, as if she is having second thoughts about her brazenness. "It's been a very long time since I felt beautiful."

I tip her face up, forcing her to look at me. "You have no idea what you do to me, do you?"

"Well, I might have a bit of an idea," she says, laughing softly. "But then I am half naked and throwing myself at you."

"Is that how you see it? Throwing yourself at me?"

"A bit, I guess. I mean, I'm older, and you're not. And-"

I don't let her finish, slipping an arm under her legs and lifting her fully up against me. We're at the shallow end of the pool, and I stride through the water as if it's the only thing between me and having this woman I want so much.

Up the steps, across the travertine floor to the glass door that opens to my bedroom. It isn't locked, and I slide it open with one hand, stepping through and leaving it open behind us. I don't stop until we're at the bed. I fling back the thick comforter and lower her slowly to the thick cotton sheets I'm suddenly glad I splurged on, kissing her now with none of the reserve I've shown her so far. I drive my tongue deep into her mouth, letting her know in no uncertain terms what else I want to do to her.

She moans softly and pulls me to her. And when I aim to slide in beside her, she steers me on top of her, one hand on each of my hips, letting me know now what she would like for me to do to her.

We kiss for a long time, wild and out of control, like two people starved for physical contact, but not just with anyone. The kind of contact that has meaning behind it. And I feel that it does. This isn't casual. It isn't thoughtless. And more than anything else, that scares the hell out of me.

I roll off her, stare at the ceiling, breathing hard, one arm thrown above my head on the pillow.

She moves onto her side, places a tentative hand on my stomach. "Hey," she says. "What is it?"

"Catherine. Dear God. There's so much you don't know about me."

"I know I want you."

I reach a hand to the side of her face, rub my thumb across her chin. I want to ignore my own misgivings, strip the rest of her clothes off and show her that all the reasons she's thought this shouldn't happen have nothing to do with how much I want her.

She leans in and kisses me softly. I feel the pleading there. She takes my hand, laces my fingers with hers. "So tell me," she says. "What else do I need to know about you? What could be so awful?"

I want to tell her. And I will. But not here. Not like this. Not so that her memories of what almost happened between us will be forever tainted by words I know she never expected to hear.

I sit up, swing my legs over the side of the bed. "I'll find your clothes and take you back to the hotel now. I'm sorry, Catherine. But it really is the best thing for you."

Chapter Twenty-seven

"All serious daring starts from within."

— Eudora Welty

Catherine

WE DRIVE BACK to the hotel in complete silence.

I keep my head turned to the night dark flowing by outside my window. I try not to think, to keep my mind blank. I pinch the palm of my left hand, willing myself not to cry. I will *not* cry in front of him. I. Will. Not.

It takes forever to get there. I feel him wanting to say something, but I don't want him to. *Please don't.* I repeat the mantra over and over in my head. It will only make it worse. There's nothing to say, anyway. All the reasons are obvious. They have been from moment one. It's not as if I didn't know that. I even tried to tell him I knew what they were.

What I don't understand is why he didn't listen before we. . .before tonight.

I squeeze my eyes shut, pinch my palm harder.

Well, it's not as if I don't know what rejection feels like. I do. But the pain from my past had at least dulled to a level that made it feel like the thing from my past that it is. But this. *This*. Somehow this is almost worse. I feel like a fool. Like a woman old enough to know better. A woman who had begun to hope for something that wasn't in the realm of possibility. Who took a shot and went for someone way out of her league.

The gate to the hotel flashes ahead in the lights of the Defender. I have never been so relieved to arrive anywhere as I am here and now.

Anders stops the vehicle at the front entrance. One of the hotel employees starts to walk around the front to get my door, but I've opened it and slid out before he can get there.

"Catherine."

I hear Anders call my name, a quiet plea, but I'm running now, through the marble foyer of the front desk, down the hallway to the stairs that lead to my room. I take them two at a time for as long as I can, and then one by one because my chest is heaving with the effort of holding back tears I can no longer hold back at all.

*

HOUSEKEEPING HAS BEEN in to do turndown service. The quiet luxury of the room is the haven I need at this moment. The heavy curtains have been pulled. A single lamp is on. I flick it off and throw myself on the bed, face down on the pillow. I consider suffocating myself with it and then stifle back a sob for the ridiculous position I have put myself in. And I have put myself there.

What was I thinking?

I'm forty years old. Started and sold a surprisingly successful company. I'm divorced. I've been cheated on. I know what heartache feels like. Why did I set myself up for more?

I roll over on the pillow, stare into the darkness, my eyes open now, tears of self-loathing streaming down my cheeks. I swipe them away, resenting the fact that they're there, and I can't stop them.

Am I a cliché? Cougar after a younger man?

I squirm on the mattress at the visual I have created for myself.

I hate the word and all its connotations. I think of the TV shows that have been created around the modern day idea of older women luring younger men to their beds, and I blush hot and hard. Or maybe it's a hot flash. Have I just catapulted myself into menopause tonight?

I sit up on the bed, run my hands through my damp hair.

Stop.

You're being ridiculous.

I think about what actually happened tonight and wonder if I am blowing it out of all proportion.

I made out with a younger guy. Check.

He decided it wasn't a good idea for us to have sex. Check.

And I have absolutely no doubt he is right.

It's not as if I've ever had an actual fling. I've been with one man in my life. My husband. Ex. Husband.

Did I really think I had it in me to do a vacation romance? A vacation fling? Whatever it would be called. Because there was never any doubt that is all it would be.

I'd be fooling myself to act as if I'm a woman who could leave this island with her heart intact after giving herself to a man like Anders.

I would have left here with my heart in tatters.

Some Cougar I am.

I wipe my hands across my eyes and realize it is time for me to go home. A two week vacation was a terrible idea anyway.

I slide off the bed, walk over to the desk and flip open the lid to my laptop. The screen is bright, and I blink against the shock to my eyes.

I type the airline into the browser and wait for my account to come up, hoping I can change my flight for tomorrow. *Please let this happen so I do not have to see him again.* I'm not sure who I'm offering the plea to but I repeat it in case anyone is listening.

Chapter Twenty-eight

"You gain strength, courage, and confidence by every experience in which you really stop to look fear in the face. You are able to say to yourself, 'I lived through this horror. I can take the next thing that comes along."

— Eleanor Roosevelt

Anders

THE HALLWAY IS endless. The lights in the ceiling overhead are so bright I squint to see my way along the corridor. I put a hand to the wall, feeling as I go.

I'm being pulled forward by a force stronger than myself. I don't want to go wherever it is taking me. I know it's somewhere terrible. But I don't have a choice. It won't let me stop. Its pull seems to be originating somewhere inside me, from the center of me. Almost as if I am pulling myself. It sounds crazy. Maybe I am crazy.

I open my eyes wider and stare as hard as I can at the end of the hallway in the far distance. I have no idea how far away it is. Or how long it will take me to get there. But I keep going. There is no option of turning around. I want to turn around. I want to go back. Behind me is the life I once had. That life is gone though. I know this as someone who has accepted the death of a loved one, knows they will never be back.

I don't know how much time passes before I get close enough to the end to see where I am going. And then I recognize the room. The chair by the window. The IV stand sitting next to it.

My heart drops. I'm sick again. The cancer is back.

I reach the doorway and stop, my gaze taking in the two dozen people sitting in loungers with IVs attached to their arms.

I search the faces, but I don't recognize anyone. All the people I had seen and met during my treatments are gone.

I wonder if they have died. A large knife of grief cuts me through the chest. I turn to run back down the corridor I've just traveled through. My feet won't let me though. They walk me forward to the chair by the window. The nurse who I remember from before is standing at its side, waiting for me. He smiles, but the smile is distorted. His face blurs before my eyes, but his voice booms in my ear. "Welcome back, Mr. Walker. Please have a seat."

There is no fight left inside me. I drop onto the chair and sit docile while he inserts the IV needle into my arm. I don't flinch at the pinch, remembering now how used to the brief pain I had gotten. I watch the drip as it begins its toxic flow into my veins.

Resignation pours through me at an equally rapid rate. I realize that I had known all along I would be back here one day. I wonder how quickly my hair will fall out this time.

I force myself to look in the mirror on the wall opposite from my chair. The same mirror I had grown to hate before. I stare hard, trying to focus in on myself. I move my head to the side, searching for my reflection. It isn't there though. I'm not there. Along with everyone I met in this room three years ago, I am gone.

*

I BOLT UPRIGHT out of sleep.

I am breathing as if I've just finished a sprint on the beach.

The room is dark, and I stare into it, trying to remember where I am.

I'm in my house. In Barbados.

I've been dreaming.

I fall back against the pillow, breathing hard, willing my mind to reject the nightmare.

It does not release me easily. Fear makes my heart pound.

I wait for it to slow, forcing myself to picture things that make me feel peaceful, hopeful. I picture the sunrise as it will look outside my house in a few hours. I picture the hatchling turtles swimming into the ocean toward their future. And I picture Catherine, the softness in her eyes when I had laid her across my bed last night.

My heart has reached a rhythm I can no longer feel against the wall of my chest. My mind has found a foothold outside the fear. But lying here, staring into the dark, I realize that I've been living a lie. Telling myself I beat the cancer. I haven't beat it at all. The possibility of its return has been dormant inside me, waiting for me to want something badly enough that it could grow out of my fear of losing the thing I want.

The thing I want is to be normal again. To let myself hope for a future. To know love and return love.

I realize that's what I want with Catherine. To give what we feel a chance.

My fear controls my life. By keeping my past a secret inside me, am I giving it power? Is that really living?

But I don't have to think about this. I already know the answer.

Chapter Twenty-nine

"We must let go of the life we have planned, so as to accept the one that is waiting for us."
—Joseph Campbell

Catherine

I WASN'T ABLE to get a flight out today. The soonest available seat is tomorrow morning at seven a.m. I'll have to get up in the middle of the night, but at this point, I don't care.

I'm up with the sunrise this morning, anyway. Sleep never fully came. I tried for a few hours, but stayed awake in a thin veil of consciousness, self-recrimination pounding in my brain, filming my skin in a heat of sweat.

I get up at five-thirty, order a pot of coffee and stand under the shower while I wait for it to come. I make the water as cold as I can stand it, letting it sluice over my face and body in a punishing assault.

I finally give myself a break and step out, wrapping one of the hotel's enormous towels around me.

I've just slipped on a thick, terry-cloth robe when the doorbell rings. I answer to the same cheerful waiter who's brought my coffee each day, and I try not to bring his mood down with my own, smiling and agreeing with his comments on the predicted brilliance of the day ahead.

But once he leaves me on the terrace with a fresh cup poured in front of me, I set my gaze on the pink-tinged skyline at the far edge of the ocean and determine that it is time for me to get back to real life. Back to doing what I do best. Running ActivGirl. At least for another two years to finish out the term I agreed to when I sold the company. Beyond that, I have no idea what my life will look like, but I feel an urgency to get my wants and hopes back under control.

I have the entire day ahead of me though. I decide to spend it on the beach, getting a last dose of Vitamin D before returning to the New York winter and the fact that my skin won't see the sun until May.

I head for the beach and my designated chair at nine. I skip breakfast, my appetite for the large buffet this morning non-existent. The friendly beach attendant gets me set up and brings me an icy bucket with a bottle of water in it. I pull the novel I'd started reading days ago from my bag and attempt to lose myself in it.

After a half-hour, I'm sweating and decide to take a dip in the ocean. I walk across the warm, white sand, my feet sinking in until I reach the packed edge. I stand for a moment and take in the beauty around me, realizing how much I will miss this place.

It feels as if I have found a spot in the world where I would love to wake up every day, retire all my winter clothes, figure out a new plan for my life. But I know that isn't reality. And that I made my choices long ago.

I wade out farther and dive in headfirst, swimming under water until I'm far enough out that I can't reach the bottom. I paddle for a bit and float face up, squinting against the sun and I close my eyes, letting it bathe my face with its heat.

I stay that way, floating. In these moments, I realize that I have grown to love this place. Love its color and warmth, the cheerful disposition of the people and the birds.

My eyes start to tear in the corners just as something touches my shoulder. I yelp and topple forward, looking for the bottom with my feet.

An arm goes around my waist and stops my struggles.

I know instantly that it is Anders.

Despite the water I am submerged in, I'm infused with heat.

He's wearing dark glasses, his eyes hidden behind them. His dark blonde hair is a little wild, as if the ocean breeze has had its way with it, and he hasn't bothered to argue.

He's shirtless, his bare chest shimmering tan in the sunlight. His skin is smooth, nearly hairless. The sight of him, the nearness of him, triggers vivid memories of what had almost happened between us, and I plant a hand at the center of his chest, pushing away from him.

He lets me go. My chin drops beneath the surface, and I inhale a gulp of salty sea-water, adding more mortification to my already too long list with Anders.

"I didn't mean to scare you," he says in a quiet voice.

I kick back a yard or so, needing the distance to scramble for composure. "What are you doing out here?" I ask, making every effort to sound as if I am staring at any other stranger on the beach.

"I wanted to talk to you."

I raise a hand. "There really is absolutely no need."

"I think the way we ended things last night said everything that needed to be said."

He reaches for my hand, pulls me toward the shore until we're both standing in water to my waist. It is only then that he says, "No. I didn't say what I needed to say."

"Anders. I get it. There's a whole list of credible reasons why last night would have been a stupid thing to do. Would you like to hear a few? Let's see. Everyone I know will accuse me of robbing the cradle when they see your young, gorgeous self. You'll think I have to have a commitment because I'm at the age of desperation. In ten years, I'll look like your—"

"Stop," he says, holding up a palm. He looks at me for several long moments before he finally says, "As far as I'm concerned, there's only one reason it would be a bad idea."

"So your reason is valid, but mine isn't."

"Four years ago, I was dying of cancer."

The words drop into the air between us, heavy with the weight of boulders launched from an airplane flying overhead. I feel as if I will drown in the tsunami wave they create. “What?” I say, barely able to hear my question.

“I’ve been okay for two years, but there are no guarantees.”

“But. . .you look so. . .”

“I’ve learned how to take care of myself. If there’s a rainbow in my experience, it’s that.”

“I’m sorry. I—”

“I’m not telling you this because I want your pity. I needed you to know that I’m not living my life like there’s a definite tomorrow. There’s today. For most people, that’s not enough.”

“Anders. I—”

He backs away. “I just needed you to know it wasn’t you.”

I watch him turn and walk out of the water, back up the beach and up the stairs to the hotel, and then he’s out of sight, gone.

Chapter Thirty

"You cannot swim for new horizons until you have courage to lose sight of the shore."
— William Faulkner

Catherine

I WALK BACK to my chair and sit for a long time, staring out at the placid ocean before me while I wonder how Anders lived the life he's described to me.

He is the picture of health. His body a testament to self-care and wellness. I think of the night in his kitchen when we had talked about diet and juicing and the importance of good food and nutrition. I had felt then that there was more beneath the surface of our conversation but brushed it off. And now I know the why.

Cancer.

The word itself is terrifying.

I think of the people I've known who have battled this horrible disease. Sadly, there have been several.

The last was a young woman named Samantha who worked in our online sales department. She was young too, early thirties. She woke up one morning with excruciating abdominal pain. She ended up in the ER only to find out she had stage four colon cancer. She went with the doctors' recommendation to use the most aggressive protocol available to her, chemo and radiation. And after three months of treatment, we thought she would be okay. She lost her hair and was so thin it was painful to see her, but she had the will to fight. I would take her soups and juices, anything I thought there was a chance of her eating. The last night I saw her, she talked of how much she wanted to get back to work, of how much she missed her old life. I wanted the same for her and believed she would have it again, eventually.

But the next morning, I received a call at the office from a mutual friend who said Samantha was in the hospital with pneumonia. I planned to go see her after work that evening, but she died an hour before I got there.

For a long time after that, I felt bitter about her death. It seemed so unfair. She wanted to live. She had so many plans. Had done so little of what she hoped to do in life.

I realized then that cancer is ruthless. That once it gets a victory in the body, it is reluctant to retreat. Temporarily, maybe. But like a rogue general in a dictator-led country, it will attempt another assault at the slightest sign of weakness.

I think of Anders now and find it almost impossible to believe that he could have been dying.

The same vibrant, strong, beautiful man who held me in his arms.

Suddenly, I am so afraid for him.

What if it comes back?

What if it has, and he doesn't know it yet?

I can't sit here any longer, torturing myself with these questions. I get up from the chair, somehow needing to outrun my own thoughts. I gather my things, walk back to the room and let myself inside the cool interior. I stand on the marble floor, letting the heat drain from my body. And then without giving myself time to change my mind, I pull on shorts and a t-shirt, grab my phone and wallet and head for the front of the hotel.

*

THE TAXI DROPS me at Needham's Point Beach. I walk the short distance to the curve of sand where we had released the hatchlings. I sit down on the sand, pulling my knees to my chest and staring out at the ocean, wondering how many of them survived. I remember what I felt watching those precious souls strike out against all odds. The way my heart hurt with hope for them as I watched them struggle with every step forward.

Had Anders' journey been like theirs, seeking out a new life for himself with all the odds stacked against him?

I somehow know that it has been. I cannot imagine the days of struggle he must have endured.

But he has survived. He's made it.

And I know that in turning me away last night, he was trying to protect me. My heart swells with hope and gratitude. But I don't want protection. I want Anders.

Chapter Thirty-one

"See how she leans her cheek upon her hand.
O, that I were a glove upon that hand
That I might touch that cheek!"
— William Shakespeare

Anders

I'M SITTING IN the living room, my gaze on the pages of a book I have not been able to focus on when I hear the doorbell ring.

The lamp on the table next to my chair is the only light on. I close the novel and consider not answering. I have no doubt that it is Catherine. I knew she would come. She has a heart. There is no question that she will try to convince me it doesn't matter.

I shouldn't let her. I know this, even as I stand and walk to the door, my hand on the wrought iron knob. I imagine her on the other side, her hand wrapped around the matching handle, and I swear I can feel the pull of her though it.

Slowly, I turn the knob, ease the door open until there is nothing between us but air.

"Hey," she says.

"Hey."

"I was in the neighborhood."

"No, you weren't."

She smiles a little and shrugs. "Okay. So I wasn't."

"Catherine—"

"May I come in?"

It's clear she isn't taking no for an answer. I step back, wave her past me. She walks in, her hands wringing nervously in front of her. There is a fine sheen of perspiration above her lip.

"Can I get you something to drink?" I ask.

"A sparkling water would be nice if you have it."

"I do. Would you like lemon with it?"

"Yes, please."

I lead the way to the kitchen and busy myself with finding the bottle of San Pellegrino, pulling a lemon from the drawer in the refrigerator and slicing it on a cutting board by the sink. I feel her eyes on me the entire time, but I don't let my gaze meet hers. It's as if to do so would be like touching a live electrical wire.

An entire book's worth of words hang between us, but I can't bring myself to open the first page.

She is the one to speak first. "I want to thank you for telling me what you told me this morning. It must not have been easy."

"I guess the truth often isn't."

"No."

Her voice is soft and low. I keep one hand on the knife and one on the lemon, not looking up as

I absorb what she has said. "Does that mean you're thanking me for letting you off the hook?"

I hear her move forward, and then her hand is on my arm. My body instantly remembers her touch, reminds me too, that I still want her.

"No," she says. "I don't mean that at all."

I put the knife down, turn to her. I fold my arms across my chest, self-defense, I guess, and say, "The last thing I want from you, Catherine, is pity."

She exhales a sigh. "Good. Because that's the last thing I have to give you."

She steps forward, presses first one hand to my chest, then the other. She keeps them there, flat, unmoving, as if she is searching for the connection we had found last night, patient in waiting for it to reestablish itself. She closes her eyes for a moment, pulls her lower lip in between her teeth and with a small sigh, looks at me directly. "If it's all we have, if you can't give me anything beyond here and now, tonight will be enough for me."

My breath collapses beneath the words, and I reach for her, hauling her in with one arm around her waist, my other hand guiding her face to mine. I kiss her with all the hunger that's been building inside me for her since the first moment I saw her. And she kisses me back as if she feels every single thing I'm feeling. Every nuance. Every heartbeat.

Her arms slide around my neck. I slip an arm under her legs, lift her up and on to the counter where she opens her legs and pulls me in.

We're both still fully clothed, but I can feel every curve of her, every line, every soft spot. An involuntary sigh of longing falls out of me, and she smiles against my mouth, putting her hand to my face. "Do you have any idea what an incredibly beautiful man you are?" she asks in a voice so low I wonder if I have imagined the question.

"Not how I see myself," I say.

"That's how I see you."

I run my hand through her wavy blonde hair, wind its length through my fingers. "I've never wanted anyone as much as I want you."

She stares at me for a moment, as if she isn't sure she should believe this. I can see that she wants to. She closes her eyes. Leans in and kisses me softly at first, and then with a deepening intensity until we are nearly wild with the need for more than just kissing, with the desire to lose the clothes that separate us.

She begins to unbutton my shirt, her fingertips grazing my skin as she goes, heightening my awareness of her with every touch. When she reaches the last button, she runs the back of her hand up the center of my chest and turns it over to place her palm over my heart. "Please, Anders."

I hear the plea beneath my name, and for a moment, a single heart-wringing moment, I ask myself if I am doing the right thing. At the same time, I realize I don't have it in me to walk away from her again. And so I put my arms around her, pick her up and walk us both straight to the bedroom, kicking the door closed behind us.

Chapter Thirty-two

"One day someone will walk into your life and make you see why it never worked out with anyone else."
— Unknown

Catherine

ANDERS IS SLEEPING.

I am exhausted. Pleasurably exhausted. Sated. Unimaginably so.

I want to sleep, but I can't. Though my body is heavy with a tiredness that needs no explanation, my mind is wide awake.

Anders is on his back. I am tucked into the curve of his arm. Our clothes are long since missing. I rest my palm on the center of his chest, absorbing the slow thud of his heart. His resting pulse is incredibly slow, but then given his level of fitness, it isn't surprising.

The curtains to the room are open just wide enough to allow a swath of moonlight to drape the top half of the bed. I raise my head to study his face, his enviably long lashes, the slash of cheekbone that is perhaps the most notable fact of his beauty.

And he is beautiful. There's not a more appropriate word that applies. I want to touch him, but I don't want to wake him. I would rather hold on to this opportunity to watch him, drink him in until I've had my fill.

But then I'm not sure I could ever tire of watching him.

As if he has felt my thoughts, his eyes open. I see his momentary confusion, and then the flare of recognition and the reality of me in his bed.

He turns onto his side, runs his hand through my hair. "Can't sleep?"

I shake my head.

"Hm." He pauses, as if thinking. "It would be rude to let you lie here with nothing to do. Don't you agree?"

"Maybe a little," I say, hearing the teasing note in his voice and injecting it in mine. "And you are, after all, a very hospitable man."

"Sooo the polite thing would be for me to find some way to entertain you, I suppose so?"

"Can't argue with your logic."

With one finger, he reaches out to trace a path along my cheek, down the center of my throat, around the curve of my breast.

I try to say something but have no air for words.

With two hands then, he spans my waist and lifts me up, as if he's doing a bench press in the gym, and slowly, slowly, lowers me on top of him. His biceps and chest get all the credit, tight and hard.

I sit straight, shocked by how instantly my body comes alive with need for him. A small sound of want escapes my lips, and I lean down to kiss him, aware of every pounding pulse beneath my skin.

"I like entertaining," he says in a low, desire-roughened voice.

"I can see why," I say softly. "You're really, really good at it."

He laughs near my ear, and his hands rove my back before settling on my bottom. He presses me to him, and then neither of us wants to talk anymore. Our bodies write their own language.

*

I HEAR ANDERS get up at an hour that feels undoable given that I feel as if I haven't slept all night. Which isn't far from true.

When I open my eyes, he's fully dressed in workout clothes. He sits on the side of the bed, leans in and kisses my forehead. "I'm going to teach. You go back to sleep. I'll be back in a bit."

"Really?" I ask. "You don't mind?"

"To the contrary. I'll spend the class picturing you waiting for me here. I'll pedal faster."

I laugh, pull the sheet up to my chin. "Okay, then. If you insist."

He brushes a hand across my hair, and then he is gone.

*

AMAZINGLY, I DO go back to sleep.

I wake to the sound of someone in the room. I raise up on one elbow and see Anders in the doorway.

"Come back to bed," I say.

"I'm a little sweaty," he says and starts to peel off his shirt. "I better get a shower first."

"One condition," I say.

"What's that?"

"Take me with you."

The look that crosses his face fills me with a power I have never in my life known. I see the effect I have on him, and I don't know that anything has ever made me happier.

He walks over to the bed, leans down and scoops me up. "No point in wasting good water," he says.

Chapter Thirty-three

"There is no instinct like that of the heart."
— Lord Byron

Anders

WE SPEND EVERY available minute of the next few days together. Along with the time we spend alone in my house, cooking, swimming and making love, I resolve to find something new to show her every day, a hike on the rugged East Coast with incredible views, a visit to the Wildlife Reserve in St. Peter to see the Green Monkeys during feeding time.

One afternoon, I make a picnic with the food I have on hand, some tomatoes and a loaf of bread I'd bought at a local bakery yesterday. I add cheese and fruit to the basket.

We load chairs and towels into the back of the Defender and head out for a beach I love going to. It's public but isn't well known, and I've wanted to show it to her. It's a twenty minute or so drive from my house, and we take the curvy roads with one of my favorite playlists from class blasting, the windows down.

The sky is so cloudless it almost looks fake as a backdrop to a bright yellow sun. I take my sunglasses off because I want to absorb all of its beauty, and then I glance at Catherine. Her head rests against the seat, and she's staring out the window at the island passing by, a look of contentment on her face that makes me happy that I might be responsible for putting it there.

It's tempting to let myself think past the here and now, wonder what lies beyond last night and today. But I'm not going to. I'm going to do what I've been doing for the past three years. Live the moment. Don't ask for more. Don't expect more.

As if she feels my thoughts, Catherine turns her head, looks directly at me. She places her hand over mine on the gearshift, squeezes once. And I don't need any words. Her touch says exactly what I'm thinking, anyway.

*

WE'RE THE ONLY ones on the beach. Late morning on a weekday, we've lucked out. On the weekends, locals make their way here, but I'm glad we've found a time to have it to ourselves. The sand is white and smooth, no rocks visible anywhere. The water is clear for at least thirty feet out where it darkens as the bottom drops off.

"It's so beautiful," Catherine says, looking over her shoulder at me. She's sitting at the edge of the water, her knees to her chest. Her hair is long and loose on her shoulders, and the look on her face is one of true appreciation that I have brought her here.

I sit down next to her, the gentle waves doing a lazy dance around our feet. "It's peaceful," I say. "The first time I came here, I felt like I'd discovered a piece of what heaven would look like."

She rests her arms on her knees and studies me for a few moments. "You've shown me a life I didn't believe was possible."

"*I* didn't think it was possible until I didn't have a choice not to go back to the life I was living."

"Was it hard to walk away?"

I hear the wistful note in her voice, as if it is something she is trying to imagine, *wants* to be able to imagine.

"No. By the time I felt like I had another chance to live, it wasn't hard at all."

"If you don't want to talk about it, please just say so."

I shake my head, wait for her to go on.

"How did you get well?"

I glance out at the ocean, set my gaze on the horizon. "I went the traditional route at first. Chemo. That's the primary treatment for leukemia. From the beginning, I hated the idea. It never made sense to me. Using poison to kill something in my body when everything else would have to be subjected to it as well."

"I can understand that," she says softly, and I can feel that she wants to touch me, but she waits, letting me go on.

"But until you've had a cancer diagnosis, you can't quite imagine the panic that takes you under like a riptide current when the doctor drops those words on you. You fight it, trying to get your head above water long enough to breathe, to think straight, but it's relentless, and you quickly figure out you have to ride whatever wave you can catch to safety. That's the one my doctor told me was my only hope to live. So I said okay. Booked the appointment. Walked into a room full of people so sick that on the first day I joined them in my designated chair, I sat with my face to the wall because if I looked at them, I couldn't stop myself from crying."

A sob escapes her throat, and I do look at her now, not bothering to hide the remembered anguish in my eyes. She slips her arm through mine, slides close so that we are touching, shoulder to hip. It's as if she wants to anchor herself to me, seal our connection so that I don't slip off into the memories I am sharing with her.

"I went there as long as I could," I finally say, my gaze again on the ocean before us. "And then one day, I knew I wasn't going to live if I went back even one more time. So I got up, pulled the needle out of my arm and left."

She's quiet for a bit, absorbing what I have said. When she speaks, her voice is raspy. "I can't imagine how much courage that took."

"I'm pretty sure it takes more courage to stay," I admit.

"What did you do then?"

"Wallowed in pity for a few days. And then at some point, realizing I had nothing to lose, I got online and started searching for other options. This place in Mexico called Sanoviv popped up in my

Facebook feed. I started reading about it, about the people who had posted their experiences, and I had to go. I didn't care if I died there. At least I would know I tried."

I see the effect my words have on her, and I regret not softening them.

"What was it like?" she asks.

"The only way I can describe it was that it felt like a place of healing. I felt it as soon as I walked through the doors. Their approach is about giving the body whatever tools they have found capable of helping the immune system mount its own attack. My treatment plan was based on giving my body the things it needed to fight the cancer. I'm embarrassed to say my diet was crap before I got diagnosed. They taught me how to eat for healing, for disease prevention."

"That's why you juice."

I nod. "I'll never stop. I actually feel guilty for all the junk I put in my body throughout my life."

"When we know better, we do better."

"Hopefully before it's too late."

"What else did they do for you?"

"A detox program. My blood work showed that I had a high level of toxins. From living in the city, I guess. We breathe in all sorts of fumes from vehicles and when we're pumping gas in our cars. Airplanes going over. I had no idea. I don't think most people have any idea. But they helped lower my levels significantly."

"That is amazing. And terrifying. What else did they do?"

"Something called Hyperthermia which aims to raise the body's core temperature for a period of time to mimic fever. When we get a fever, it's the body's way of trying to kill whatever is making us sick."

"But I've always heard you should take something to lower a fever."

"If it gets above a certain point, my understanding is yes. Lower fevers are one of our body's weapons."

"I had no idea."

"Me either before I went there."

She looks at me then, and says, "I'm so grateful you found that place."

"I wouldn't be here if I hadn't. I do know that much."

She reaches for my hand, laces her fingers through mine. We sit for a while, the waves making the only sound around us until she finally says, "And I have no idea how I found you. But I'm glad I did."

Chapter Thirty-four

"In his blue gardens men and girls came and went like moths among the whisperings and the champagne and the stars."

— F. Scott Fitzgerald

Catherine

IT'S LIKE A day out of a movie I might have written for myself featuring all of my most hoped-for fantasies. I'm on the most beautiful beach I've ever seen with a gorgeous man who also happens to be kind and smart and looks at me as if he can only barely restrain himself from making love to me right here under a sky as blue as any I've ever seen.

Not that I would mind. Except for modesty and the fact that there would be no hiding the fact that I am older than he is in this light. Except for that.

We eat the amazing lunch he has prepared, sitting on towels beneath a bright yellow umbrella with our toes in the sand.

I'm so full I have to stop. "I need a one-piece after

that," I say, holding my stomach. "No hiding this belly now."

He laughs. "What belly?"

"I'll just keep it sucked in," I say. "Don't mind me if I can't talk."

He shakes his head, still smiling. "You look incredible."

"If I did your spin class every day, I would look incredible."

He slides onto his side, props himself up on one elbow. "So stay here, and you can do it every day."

I sober beneath the suggestion. "I wish," I say, failing to conceal the longing in my voice.

"You don't have to wish. It's your life. And we only get one."

I consider what he has said, curbing what would have normally been an automatic response outlining my responsibilities at ActivGirl. But I stop myself because I realize for the first time in my life, they aren't automatic at all.

*

WE SPEND THE afternoon swimming in the beach's u-shaped cove, alternately floating in the water and lazing in the sun.

It's almost four o'clock when I turn my face to his where he is lying on his stomach, his head on his crossed forearms. "This might be the most perfect day of my life."

"Mine too," he says in a low voice, as if he's a little afraid to admit it.

I put my hand on his shoulder. It's hot from the

sun, the muscles beneath my palm defined and taut. "Can we stay here forever?"

"I will if you will."

I smile, shrug, as if I was kidding all along. "Why is it that I came here with vacation as the temporary thing, and all of a sudden, I'm wondering how I can go back to cold and twelve hour workdays?"

"Then don't."

"If only it were that easy."

"It is easy when you let yourself admit that life is actually very short. We don't have forever to do the things that make us happy."

"I have two more years on my contract."

He considers this for a bit and then says, "You could buy your way out."

The words drop between us, my immediate instinct to deny their plausibility. But I can't make myself say it because all of a sudden, I'm wondering what if? Could I? Would I?

The questions propel me off the towel and across the sand, where I run into the water, not stopping until I am waist deep and diving straight in. I swim out as far as I can go, trying not to think about the fact that my strokes are anything but graceful. When I finally come to a stop, I am breathing hard and treading water.

"Hey."

I jump at the touch on my shoulder, whirling to find Anders treading beside me.

"You don't have to run away," he says. "I didn't really think you would say yes."

I look at him for a stretch of silence before I finally admit, "The thing is I really want to."

And with that, he hooks an arm around my waist and pulls me to him. I anchor my legs around his hips, my arms around his neck and kiss him with all the heat and longing welling up inside me. In a little while, he takes my hand and swims us both back to the beach where it is a really good thing there is no one else around.

Chapter Thirty-five

"You'd have to have personally been trapped and felt flames to really understand a terror way beyond falling."
— David Foster Wallace

Nicole

THE LAPTOP SITS on the table in the apartment's small kitchen. She opens the lid and clicks on the email provider, waiting while the icon circles and opens. She hits Compose and types in her mom's email address. She clicks on the body of the message.

She picks up her phone and opens the Notes app. Inside the Passwords folder, she scrolls down to the short list of accounts that represent the financial status of her life. There aren't many. But for the few she has, she types each one into the email. Bank name. Routing number. Account number.

She types in her login info for the bank's website, double-checking the password.

She scans her Notes for the name of her insurance

company, finds it near the bottom of the list and types that in too.

She logs in into her bank account, waiting for the password to register. Once inside, she clicks on checking – there's nothing in savings – and frowns at the abysmal balance. Enough to pay her bills, anyway. She makes an electronic payment for the past month's electricity. She pays the rent on her apartment with a check – it's five days late – tucks it inside an envelope, seals it and puts a stamp in the right-hand corner. The cable bill is also due. She pays that online with her checking account, and by the time she's done, the balance is $9.97.

Sad to think that's what's left of a lifetime of work through age thirty-eight, but that is the reality of it and further proof that her decision is the right one.

A Facebook notification pops up on the screen. She clicks and makes it go away. Facebook is for people with things to show the world they are proud of, grateful for. Nicole has nothing to be proud of, and for the things she was once grateful for, she has destroyed any hope of ever having them again.

She closes the laptop, and if she had expected to feel sad, she doesn't. Finally, she knows she is making a choice that will be for the good of everyone in her life. She has not made it lightly, but she knows it is the right one.

Secure in this truth, she turns off the lights in the kitchen, flicks off the lamps in the small living room, walks into her bedroom and closes the door with a quiet but final click.

Chapter Thirty-six

"Every man has his secret sorrows which the world knows not; and often times we call a man cold when he is only sad."

— Henry Wadsworth Longfellow

Catherine

THE PHONE WAKES me.

My ringtone is Church Bells, and the dong, dong, dong, rouses me with the thought that I am in Florence, Italy. I chose the sound because it is a good memory, a time in my twenties when Nicole and I did a rail pass across Italy and France. We had both loved coming awake to the chorus of church bells audible through a cracked window.

I turn over, force my eyes open. Is it morning?

But as I raise up on one elbow, feeling the warmth of Anders sleeping next to me, I come back to where I am. I have the horrible realization that something is wrong. I fumble for the phone, trying to focus on the lit screen. The time says 1:55 AM above my mom's cell number.

Suddenly anxious, I tap the answer icon. "Mom? Are you okay? Is Dad—"

But my mother cuts me off before I can finish. "Catherine." She cannot go on beyond this, her sobs robbing her of words.

"What is it, Mom? You're scaring me."

By now, Anders is awake too. He is sitting up, his hand on my shoulder.

My mother's crying is unlike anything I have ever heard from her. It is the gut-wrenching sound of a broken heart. Tears stream down my face. "Mom, what is it?"

"I'm in the airport on the way to West Palm Beach. Your sister is in the hospital there." An awful, long silence follows the words. And then, "Oh, Cat. Dear God. She tried to kill herself tonight."

"What?"

The word falls out of me. My mind goes blank. I cannot process what she has said. Anders' arm slips around my shoulders. He pulls me into the circle of his embrace. And he's holding me tight, as if he knows I am going to fall apart.

"Is she. . .is she going to be all right?"

"The only doctor I've spoken to said it is too soon to know." She stops there, breathes in an audible intake of air. Silence beats through the phone before she finally adds, "They've pumped her stomach. She took an overdose of antidepressant. He said it will be days before we can know the long-term effects."

Again, she cannot go on, her crying the only sound coming through the phone.

"Mom." My voice breaks across the utterance, as if I am reaching out to latch onto her. "Is Dad with you?"

"Y-yes. Of course."

"I'll be there as soon as I can get a flight." I have no idea if Mom knows where I am. I didn't tell her about this trip. Guilt attacks me like a knife in the back. I draw in a sharp breath, try to focus on what matters right now. "Will you text me the name of the hospital?"

"Yes. Be safe, Cat." And with that, she is gone.

In the instant silence that surrounds us, I cannot bring myself to look at Anders. Questions fly through my mind at a thousand miles an hour.

"Don't," he says, pressing a kiss to the top of my head.

I know exactly what he means, but how can I not? I shake my head, whisper, "What if it's too late?"

He hugs me tighter, but doesn't answer. Despite our age difference, both of us have reached a point in life where we understand the futility of denying truth. And the truth is I may not ever have the opportunity to forgive my sister. If that is true, how will I ever forgive myself?

Chapter Thirty-seven

"If you are not too long I will wait here for you all my life."
— **Oscar Wilde**

Anders

I SIT IN the Defender, watching her walk into the airport, pulling her suitcase behind her. She'd asked me not to come inside. Even though I'd wanted to, wanted those extra minutes standing next to her, I did as she asked.

The sun is barely up. There was one first-class seat left on the 7 AM flight to Miami. As soon as she'd hung up with her mother, I'd gotten out of bed and started looking for a flight. I have to believe there was serious intervention taking place on her part. The unlikelihood of getting a flight that would allow her to rent a car in Miami and get to West Palm by early afternoon was enough to make me sure of it. I'm thankful for that, even though I know as she disappears into the airport that she will not return.

She never said the words, but I read it in her face, in the way she couldn't meet my eyes. More than anything, I wanted to tell her how much I want her to come back. But somehow I know that her memory of me will be tangled with this news of her sister and her own guilt about their relationship. I don't want that. The only choice I have is to let her go.

As I pull away from the airport, the Defender growling a low protest as it changes gears, all I feel is a bone-deep sense of grief, for Catherine's sister, for the two of us and what might have been.

Chapter Thirty-eight

"Between too early and too late, there is never more than a moment."
— Franz Werfel

Catherine

I STARE OUT the window of the plane at the clouds below. My thoughts are a jumbled fog of questions and self-ridicule and regret.

Some part of me thinks it can't be true. How could Nicole try to take her own life? Is this my fault? Am I responsible?

I try to figure out when my sister would have made such a decision. Was it suddenly? Had she been planning it for a long time? Was it because I didn't answer her birthday email?

A hand touches my shoulder. I jump and turn my head to find a stewardess smiling at me. "Would you like something to drink? Coffee, tea?"

"Coffee, please," I say automatically, although my stomach lurches at the thought of food. Maybe the caffeine will give my brain the ability to make sense of the phone call from my mother. And the awful, awful realization that I may not make it in time. That Nicole may die before I get there.

I lean my head against the seat and close my eyes.

I think of how things have been between my sister and me for the past three years. Of the anger I was certain had rusted a hole inside the center of my once bottomless love for her.

But somehow, since the moment I ended the call with my mom, I have only been able to think of Nicole as we were before three years ago. Before Connor. I remember us as little girls, the way Nicole wanted to do anything I did. I picture her following me through our house, her love-worn doll Emmy tucked under her arm. It didn't matter what I was doing or where I was going. Nicole just wanted to be a part of it.

Was I a nice older sister? Or did I take advantage of her devotion to me?

I wonder now, as I have wondered many times in the past three years, why Nicole chose Connor. Was it about taking something from me? Or was it my sister never having enough faith in her own ability to make her way, to trust her choices? She had always tried to follow mine. In some convoluted way, was picking Connor just more of that?

Should I have seen that before now? Before Nicole decided life wasn't worth living anymore?

A sob rises up in my throat and I lean forward in my seat, wrapping my arms around my waist and pressing my lips together.

Please, God. Please give us a chance to fix this. Please don't let her die. Please. Please give me another chance.

Chapter Thirty-nine

"Believe that life is worth living and your belief will help create the fact."
— William James

Nicole

IT'S DARK.

She stumbles, hands out in front her, trying to find something solid to latch onto. But the darkness is like she imagines space must be. Billions of miles of universe with planets so far apart that there is no hope of falling into one. Still, she tries, grappling, reaching out, staring so hard for any speck of light that it feels as if her eyes might pop from her head.

There's a voice. A woman. And another. A man. Younger.

She tries to focus on their conversation, but at first it sounds like a foreign language she's never heard before. Sentences uttered so fast she cannot make out the individual words. One breaks through. ICU.

ICU. Who's in the ICU?

Fear lashes at her. Is it one of her parents? Catherine?

As if the conversation has been slowed down for her own comprehension, she understands more of what the voices are saying. Front desk nurse. Predicting an ICU patient dead by morning. This one. Organ donor.

Confusion drowns her brain. Maybe she blacks out. When she becomes aware again, she is wondering who they were talking about.

A hand touches her arm. *Nicole. Nicole.* It's her mother's voice. Saturated with tears. *Nicole, please wake up. It's Mama. I'm here.*

Pain consumes her. She wants to go to her mother. She tries to run, but her legs are stuck in something. It feels like quicksand, and it is pulling her down, down, back into the blackness. But just before her head goes completely under, she realizes who the voices were talking about. The patient expected to be dead by morning. The organ donor.

They were talking about her.

Chapter Forty

"I'd rather regret the things I've done than the things I haven't done."
—Lucille Ball

Catherine

I GRAB AN Uber at the airport. The quickest one is the most basic, but I don't care. With me and my suitcase stuffed in his backseat, I urge the college student to get his economy car to the hospital in West Palm Beach as quickly as possible. He takes I-95 and pushes the small vehicle toward eighty. The car shakes, but we're taking the hospital exit within a few minutes, and I appreciate his focus on getting me there.

When he pulls up at the entrance, I thank him and slide out of the backseat, pulling my suitcase behind me. Inside, I ask the volunteer at the front desk which room my sister is in and then ask if I can leave my luggage with her. She starts to tell me she's not supposed to do that, but maybe it's the distraught look on my face that makes her change her mind. I pull the case behind the desk, make sure it is out of her way and then bolt for the elevator.

Nicole is in the ICU on the twelfth floor. I wait for each numbered level to slide by, each one ticking by in synch with the pulse in my throat. The doors finally open, and I step onto the waxed white floor, looking left and then right for the ICU signs. It's to the right. I walk quickly down the hall, following the arrows to a pair of red doors marked **INTENSIVE CARE UNIT. No more than one visitor allowed at a time. Ring buzzer for admittance.**

My hand is on the buzzer when I hear my name and turn to find my mother walking toward me with tears streaming down her face. My composure melts, and I let myself be folded into her arms, each of us holding onto the other as if we've been dropped in the middle of the ocean and must not let go if we are to survive.

Finally, she leans back and pushes a strand of tear-soaked hair from my face. "How is she?" I ask, the words barely audible under my fear of hearing the answer.

My mom shakes her head, glancing down and then meeting my gaze with tear-drenched eyes. "Not good. She's so lucky they found her."

"Who? Who found her?"

"There was a fire alarm in her building. The firefighters were going door to door to find the problem. If they hadn't gone in to check her apartment, no one would have found her in time."

A sob rises out of me at the image of Nicole dying alone. I think of the last time I saw her, a weekend a few months ago when I went to South Carolina to visit my parents. She'd been so happy to have me there, and even though she'd questioned me about the divide she sensed between Nicole and me, we had mostly avoided the subject and done the things Mom liked to do when I was home, visit aunts and uncles, go to the library on Saturday morning where she enlisted my help picking out a few novels to read. Go to church on Sunday morning and have as many relatives as possible over for lunch afterwards.

She had looked so happy that weekend and always young for her age. But this weight that has been dropped on her, Nicole's attempt to take her own life, has aged my mother overnight. I feel instant grief, fear stabbing me at the thought of losing her as well as Nicole.

"Oh, mom. She'll be okay. She has to be."

My voice breaks, and I press my face to her shoulder the way I used to do as a little girl, and I dreaded telling her something I had done wrong. As if she feels the awful burden weighing on me, she pulls back and says, "What is it, Cat? I know something happened between you and Nicole, but neither of you has been willing to tell me. Do you think I haven't sensed the divide between you two?"

Reluctant as I am to meet her knowing gaze, I pull back, meet my mother's eyes. "I don't want to tell you now, Mom. I promise I will, but it doesn't feel right now. All that matters is that Nicole gets through this."

Mom wants to know the truth, but she nods once, and says, "Go in and see her. We can only visit one at a time. I'll wait out here. Just go through the doors, and the nurse at the desk will take you to her."

Here, I falter. The thought of seeing Nicole alone fills my feet with concrete, and I can't bring myself to move.

"Go on, honey. She needs to know you're here."

Tears fill my eyes, and I want to sob out the truth. That it is my inability to forgive my sister that is the reason she is here.

*

THE NURSE IS a woman in her fifties who has clearly seen more sadness than any human should have to process. I see this in her eyes as she puts a hand on my shoulder and directs me down a short hallway to the bed where my sister lies, still as death.

"She's in a coma, as you know," she says, her voice soft and sympathetic.

"Can she hear us?" I ask.

"Many people think the answer to that is yes."

"What do you think?" I look at her, wanting to see her answer as well as hear it.

"I've had patients tell me they did have awareness when they were unconscious. And I have to say, there were some memories voiced to me that I knew to be accurate."

I don't know whether to feel comforted by this or alarmed by the thought that Nicole might be aware of where she is and what has happened to her.

"I try to tell family," the nurse says, empathy underlining her words, "that the important thing is to just be present. Let them know you're here. Sit with her. The doctors are limiting her visits to fifteen minutes. I'll be back, okay?"

I nod, trying to thank her, but I can't make any words come out. She walks away, heading back down the hallway to the front desk.

It is only when I am alone that I let myself fully look at my sister. I cannot stop the sob that rises up out of me. I sit, collapse, onto the chair next to the bed. Her skin is so pale it is as if all the blood has been drained from her body. Her arms lie to her sides, her palms flat against the mattress. The tube inserted in her mouth is hooked to a machine that helps her breathe. The sound it makes is a soft *whoosh-risp*, over and over again, that reminds me with each intake that it is the machine keeping her alive.

I sit, staring at her. Not a single word comes to me. The only thing that comes to my mind is *Why*? Why have you done this to yourself? Why did you betray me?

They are not questions I can ask. I reach for her hand, lace her cold fingers through mine. There is something in the connection between us, her skin against mine, that melts the awful rock of anger in my heart. I drop my head and begin to cry. I hold her hand as tight as I dare, and finally, the words come. "Nicole. Come back. Please. Don't go like this. I need you. We'll find a way back. Don't. Go. You're my sister. I forgive you."

Chapter Forty-one

'When you are Real you don't mind being hurt.'
'Does it happen all at once, like being wound up,' he asked, 'or bit by bit?'
'It doesn't happen all at once,' said the Skin Horse. 'You become. It takes a long time. That's why it doesn't happen often to people who break easily, or have sharp edges, or who have to be carefully kept. Generally, by the time you are Real, most of your hair has been loved off, and your eyes drop out and you get loose in the joints and very shabby. But these things don't matter at all, because once you are Real you can't be ugly, except to people who don't understand."
— Margery Williams Bianco, The Velveteen Rabbit

Catherine

MY DAD IS waiting beside my mom when I come out of the ICU. The nurse who had shown me in had kindly, but firmly, told me I would have to leave when my allotted time was up. I could see that she would let me stay had it been up to her, but I didn't want to put her in that position.

As soon as my dad sees me, he starts to cry, and then I'm crying, too, and we're all hugging each other, our arms forming a circle of support like pillars under a bridge.

I can't remember if I've ever seen my dad cry, and the sound of his broken heart deepens the cracks in my own. It's then I know I have to tell them the truth about what happened between Nicole and me. I don't want to, but they deserve to know that I have a part to play in the reason she is here.

I pull back and look at them both. "Can we go somewhere private? There's something I have to tell you."

"Of course, honey," Dad says in a shaky voice.

Mom leads the way down the hall and to the far end of the corridor where a small waiting area is marked for visitors of ICU patients. There's no one else there, and as we step inside, I close the door behind us.

"What is it, Cat?" Mom asks, and I can see she is worried there is something more horrible to absorb, and maybe there is. One daughter who no longer wants to live. And another with a heart of stone.

I walk over to the window and look out across the road between the hospital and the water. I fold my arms across my chest, not sure I can hold back the dam of remorse waiting to spill out of me. The silence in the room becomes so loud that I have to get the words out. They are poison in my soul. "It's my fault she's here."

I say the words without turning around. I can't face them.

My mom's voice is a whisper. "What do you mean, honey?"

My dad walks over, puts his hand on my shoulder and slowly turns me to face them. "Catherine. You love your sister. You've always loved her."

A sob rises in my throat, and I can no longer keep it inside me. "We haven't talked to each other in a long time. . .something happened."

"What?" Mom implores. The agony in her voice makes me realize I can no longer keep any of it from them. Maybe I should have told them long ago. Maybe they could have helped Nicole and me find our way back.

"Connor and Nicole had an affair."

My dad takes a step back and drops onto a chair by the window. Neither of us says anything, the silence in the room thick with shock.

I wait for them to absorb what I have said. There is nothing to add to soften it. The truth is an ugly fact.

"Oh, Cat," Mom says. "Why?"

I shake my head. "It doesn't matter now. Obviously, Connor and I had problems I didn't recognize."

"How could they?" Mom's voice is a sob.

"I don't know," I admit on a broken note. "But is my sin of unforgiveness worse than their sin of betrayal? That's the question I've been asking myself."

"Catherine," my dad says, disbelief underlining my name. "No one would blame you."

"I blame me. She's reached out to me numerous times. Asked me to forgive her."

My mom starts to cry again. She walks to the window and stares out, her shoulders shaking.

I wish I knew what to say to comfort her. My dad. Myself. Forty years on this earth, and there is something I know with complete certainty. There are things that happen to us for which there simply is no comfort to be had.

*

THE NEXT TWENTY-FOUR hours seem more like months. I stay at the hospital, make use of the family shower available on the ICU floor and sleep in the waiting room, going in to see Nicole whenever the nurses will allow me. I insist that Mom and Dad go to their hotel and get some sleep. They both look exhausted.

It's almost six p.m. when they leave. I've assured Mom I will get something to eat from the cafeteria downstairs, but as I sit staring at the TV screen with a muted news channel glaring back at me, I feel sick at the thought of food.

My phone beeps, and I reach for it, glancing at the screen. Anders' name makes my heart drop. I have purposefully blocked my mind of any thoughts of him. The darkness of this place and the reason I'm here overshadows Barbados and everything that happened there. Part of me wonders if it actually happened at all.

I tap into Messages and then on Anders' name.

I can't stop thinking about you. How is your sister?

I consider what to say. Every response that comes to mind sounds trivial.

She is the same. No change yet. Thank you for asking.
How are you?
I'm okay.
Really?

I start to type. Stop.

Catherine. I want to come there. Be with you.

Reading the words, a sob rises out of my chest and spills into the silent room. The thought of having Anders here, burying myself in the circle of his arms is a comfort I do not deserve. I don't deserve *him*.

My fingers type before I can let my heart change my mind.

What we had was wonderful. But it wasn't something that could last. We both know that. I don't know how the days we had together convinced me what we had was real. It felt real. But my life is here. Escape isn't an option. I wish only the best for you, Anders. I won't be coming back there. It's better that we say goodbye now. I'm not the woman for you. I'm sorry.

I exit out of the message app, the screen blurring in front of my eyes. I turn off the phone and put it away.

Chapter Forty-two

"For after all, the best thing one can do when it is raining is let it rain."

— Henry Wadsworth Longfellow

Anders

SOME PART OF me knows she is right.

What I had with Catherine fits every definition of a vacation romance.

She came to Barbados for a temporary escape from a very demanding life. I knew that up front. I live in a place that is fantasy to most. A temporary escape at best.

That's what it was for Catherine. Reality for her is a successful business in which she still plays a vital role. And I know she will blame herself for her sister's suicide attempt. I truly hope that is what it turns out to be. An attempt.

I want to go to her, break down the walls she is building around her own desire for happiness. But the timing is wrong. I don't want her memories of me, her vision of what we could have been, to be woven into the fabric of the pain she is going through.

What choice is there then but to accept what she is asking of me?

Chapter Forty-three

"Keep your face always toward the sunshine – and shadows will fall behind you."
— Walt Whitman

Catherine

IT'S THE END of Nicole's second week in the hospital. There has been no change in her condition. She is unresponsive to all stimulus, doesn't respond to our pleas for her to wake up. Her stare seems to see a thousand miles away, and I despair that she will never come back.

Mom and Dad have gone downstairs for a cup of coffee when I go in for my fifteen minute visit with Nicole. I'm sitting in a chair next to her bed, massaging the palm of her left hand when Doctor Lewis comes in to check on her for morning rounds. He's a nice enough man who looks overworked. His gray hair is a little too long, as if he hasn't taken the time for a haircut in a while. I've formed the impression that he cares about his patients. There are just too many of them. He greets me with a quick good morning and a perfunctory, "Any changes you've noticed?"

I wish I could say yes, wish for any sign, however small, that Nicole is getting better. "No." I draw in a deep breath and say, "What are the chances, Dr. Lewis, that Nicole will wake up from this?"

He lifts the sheet from the bottom of the bed and traces a pen-like instrument down the sole of each of her feet. There is no response. He pulls the sheet back down, looks at me with a resignation I wish I did not see in his eyes. "A true coma usually doesn't last more than three to four weeks. We're at two and a half for Nicole, so I haven't given up hope yet."

My heart flutters, settles. "What happens after four weeks?"

He's quiet for a moment, and then in a matter-of-fact voice, says, "The patient dies. Or transitions into what we call a vegetative state or the patient regains varying degrees of consciousness."

I absorb his honest explanation, trying to picture Nicole remaining this way for the rest of her life, and I can't bear the thought of it. My voice is shaky when I ask, "Do you think it is still possible she will regain consciousness?"

"Anything is possible, dear," he answers kindly. "I've been in practice long enough to know that we doctors do not have all the answers. The human body is resilient, but I have to be honest with you. Your sister's overdose would have killed her if she hadn't been found when she was. She meant for her effort to succeed."

The words slice through me with their obvious truth. It is impossible to deny.

"And here's something to think about," he says in a somber voice. "If she does pull through, her will to live will have to be different than it was when she made the decision to take her life. I have seen families devastated when their loved one survives only to succeed at a later date."

The revelation is a sobering one. Somehow, I've been thinking only of her pulling through. And that if she does, it would mean everything is better. I realize that isn't true at all.

Dr. Lewis places a hand on my shoulder, squeezes once, and then he leaves the room. I sit in somber silence, staring at my sister's face, barely recognizable with the tubes in her mouth and nose. I take her hand in mine again, drop my forehead onto the mattress of the bed, sobs shaking through me. I try to stifle their sound, but I cannot. My grief is unbearable because not only am I mourning the loss of the sister who was once my best friend, I cannot deny my culpability in the desperate place Nicole must have been in that last night.

"Nic." Her name breaks from my lips, and suddenly, I am pleading with her. "Please come back. Please give me another chance. Please don't go like this. I'm sorry. I'm so sorry. I should have forgiven you. I do forgive you. Come back to us. We'll find our way. Just. Come. Back."

My tears fall onto our hands, mine clasped tight with hers. All of a sudden, I go completely still, raising my head to stare at Nicole. I felt something.

Not a complete squeeze of my hand, but something. My heart races with hope. I know, somehow, I know, my sister has understood me.

Chapter Forty-four

"To die, to sleep –
To sleep, perchance to dream – ay, there's the rub,
For in this sleep of death what dreams may come..."
— William Shakespeare

Nicole

SHE SEES HERSELF from above.

She is terrified because it's as if she's seen someone who looks just like her, and she is obviously not well. There is no denying that the woman lying on the bed with all the tubes protruding from her body is her. The sobbing woman next to the bed is Catherine.

She sees all of this from above the bed, as if she is suspended in the air or has a peephole in the ceiling. Her heart feels like someone is squeezing it hard enough to take her breath away. She wants to reach out, reassure her sister she is here with her. But is she?

She tries to speak, but she can't hear her voice. She wants to go to Catherine, comfort her. Her feet are in quicksand, and even as she tries to pull them out, she sinks lower. With every effort, she feels more of her body disappear into the depths below. She calls for her sister, but she isn't sure whether her voice is audible. She knows she is sinking deeper and deeper. In a moment, she will be under. If she can just keep her head up long enough to let Catherine know how sorry she is. "Catherine!"

She hears her own scream, but her sister hasn't heard her at all. She continues to cry, heartbroken. Then the quicksand takes her under altogether, and her chance melts to ether.

Chapter Forty-five

"Not knowing when the dawn will come
I open every door."
— Emily Dickinson

Anders

IT'S ALMOST SEVEN P.M. The sky is turning dark with just a hint of pink sunlight tinting its edges. I slide out of the Defender in the parking area just off Needham's Point Beach. A few other vehicles are parked nearby. Hannah Brathwaite texted earlier this afternoon to ask if I wanted to help with a baby turtle release. It's something I always enjoy being a part of, but something in me had resisted the thought of going. I knew being here would remind me of Catherine, and it does.

Hannah waves from farther down the beach, and I walk toward her, determined to see this amazing miracle with the same appreciation with which I have always seen it.

"Hey," she says, walking over to give me a hug. "How are you?"

"Good," I say. "You?"

"Nervous."

"How many?"

"Fifty-six."

"That's good."

"Every one counts." She pulls back to give me a long look. "Where's your friend Catherine?"

I hesitate and answer truthfully. "She's no longer here."

"Ah," she says softly. And then, "I had the impression she might stay."

"Would have been nice," I admit.

"Did you ask her to?"

I attempt lightness even as I hear myself fail the attempt. "She has another life she had to get back to."

"Umm, I had the feeling she was pretty taken with you, Anders. And you looked happy with her."

"I could have been," I admit.

Hannah takes my hand, leads me over to the trays where the baby turtles are waiting for their release. She bends over, picks one up. "Life is short, my friend. We have to make the most of our chances. We're not so different from these little guys. Happiness is out there. But it's not guaranteed, and we can't wait for it to come to us."

She sets the little guy down, and he starts out across the sand, heading for the ocean. We both kneel next to the tray of babies and gently lift them out, one at a time. They instantly set off after the first one, instinct telling them what to do.

Watching them, my heart tightens with hope for them all. And as the last few dip into the small waves at the edge of the beach, I understand clearly what I can learn from them.

Chapter Forty-six

"Yea, I shall return with the tide."
— Khalil Gibran

Nicole

SHE SEES THE light and walks toward it. Thoughts flit through her mind, but she can't grasp on to any of them. They are elusive like the lightning bugs she and Catherine used to try to catch on summer nights when they were little.

The light is so bright it hurts to look into it. She tries to open her eyes wider, but the glare hurts, and she squints against it. She wants to raise her hand to shield her eyes. The effort seems monumental, like dragging a sled full of rocks uphill. But she's pretty sure she's moved it a little so she keeps trying.

"Nicole."

Catherine's voice. She sounds both close and far away at the same time. Nicole attempts to answer but her lips won't move.

"Nic! You moved your hand. Can you hear me?"

Her sister's voice is frantic. She wants her to answer, and she so wants to do this for her.

Where am I?

The question screams through her mind as if she's said it out loud, but she doesn't think she has. It's too muffled, trapped.

But then she feels her hand being held, squeezed. "Nicole." Her sister's voice. Her sister's hand stroking her cheek.

"Cat."

She hears the sound of her own warbled voice and knows she has managed to utter the name out loud. And then her sister is sobbing, the sound both broken and joyful. That is the moment she realizes she has crossed the threshold between the dark and the light.

Chapter Forty-seven

"Anger is an acid that can do more harm to the vessel in which it is stored than to anything on which it is poured."

— Mark Twain

Catherine

THE THING ABOUT second chances is knowing what to do with them if they're given to you.

In the hours following Nicole's awakening, I watch my parents cry with relief even as I realize their joy is tangled up with the same thorny questions encumbering my own. Will Nicole be the same as she was before the coma? Will she feel the same despair that led her to make the choice she made? Can I drown my own feelings of betrayal with the gratitude I feel to have her back?

The only question I can answer for myself is the last one. That is the only one I have any control over at all. As I stand at the foot of my sister's bed, watching my mom hold her hand and speak to her in a soft voice, I decide once and for all that I will put the past behind me. Completely. Irrevocably. I don't want to be the person who chooses not to do that. Who chooses bitterness as the pill I swallow each day.

Dr. Lewis has told us only time will reveal the damage caused by Nicole's overdose. Only time will tell how fully she will recover.

Three days pass before Nicole speaks more than a word or two. I've found it hard to know what to say and have let my mom and dad be the reason I stand back and say little. But finally the time comes when I'm left alone with my sister. She has been moved to a room that is a step down from ICU, and we are allowed to visit as long as we like. Mom and Dad have gone downstairs to get something to eat, and I'm sitting next to Nicole's bed, watching her sleep.

When she opens her eyes, tears seep from the corners, and I realize she hasn't been asleep at all.

"I don't deserve to have you here," she says in a voice that sounds like a rusty replica of hers.

I reach for her hand, clasp it between my own. I lean forward until my forehead is resting on our joined hands. I try to speak but the words stick in my throat. When I finally lift my head, Nicole is staring at me, her eyes filled with a remorse that twists my heart. "I'm so sorry, Cat."

"I know," I say.

"I wish I could redo all of it."

"There's plenty I wish I could redo," I say. "I shut you out. I'm so sorry for that."

"I don't blame you."

"I blame me."

"Catherine, you're not the one who did wrong."

"I closed my heart to you. That's wrong."

Fresh tears slide down Nicole's face. "Next to mom and dad, there's no one who matters more to me. I don't know how I could hurt you the way I did."

A canyon of silence hangs between us.

"Why did you?"

The question is out before I can stop myself from asking. I'm immediately filled with remorse and wish I could take it back.

"I've asked myself so many times," Nicole says in a barely audible voice. "The only answer I have is that I've always wanted to be you. You've always been the better version of me."

I sit back in my chair, shocked by what my sister has just said. "Nicole. That's not true."

"It is true," she says, sadness tinging the words. "It's not an excuse. Nothing excuses what I did. If I'm honest though, maybe I thought it would be nice to be wanted by someone the way Connor always wanted you. I think I believed if he wanted me as much as he wanted you, that would mean I was as good as you."

"Nicole."

My voice cracks in half, and I swallow back the sob pushing its way up from my throat.

Tears well up, slide down her cheeks. "I know it's awful, Cat. What I did is inexcusable. Unforgivable. And you were a good sister to me. It's not your fault that I felt like less. You never tried to make me feel that way. Everything that happened is my fault."

"I wasn't a perfect sister," I say. "I know that. There were times when I took you for granted. But I loved you. And—"

"I betrayed you."

I could deny it, but nothing really makes sense to me except being willing to look at the truth. "It felt that way. But where there's love, there should be forgiveness. I should have forgiven you, Nicole."

Nicole starts to cry then, bone deep sobs pouring out of her. "I don't deserve it."

I sit on the edge of the bed, put my arms around her, pull her tight against me. "Yes," I say. "You do deserve it. And I forgive you. I want you back, Nic. I've missed you. I've missed us."

Nicole presses her face to my shoulder. Her tears wet my blouse.

Minutes pass, and Nicole goes limp, silent. And then she slips her arms around me, hugs me back. So hard that I cannot take a deep breath.

That's how our parents find us. I look up to see Mom and Dad standing in the doorway, their faces lit with relief and joy. I hold out a hand. They walk over and circle us both with their arms. And for the first time in a very long while, it feels as if we might finally have a chance to be whole again.

Chapter Forty-eight

"That is one good thing about this world…there are always sure to be more springs."
— L.M. Montgomery

Catherine

OVER THE NEXT two days, Nicole and I pour our hearts out to each other. We say things we should have said long ago, airing hurts and slights until we finally reach what feels like the bottom of them. Once we're done, it feels as if the painful stuff has been purged, and we can navigate our way back to what was once good between us. And we start to talk about the old times, crazy stuff we did as kids, climbing trees we shouldn't have climbed, sneaking into a neighbor's barn so we could play with the baby chicks. And the times we tried our parents' patience to breaking point, the dumb stuff we did as teenagers when we thought we knew everything there was to know.

The first time Nicole smiles, I feel as if a storm-dark sky has been penetrated by a ray of sun, and there is hope that we might have sunny days ahead. They won't all be that way. Life isn't like that. I'm old enough to accept this. But the good days are worth the bad ones we endure. And while I've had plenty of friends I value and appreciate, family is different. Nicole and I have a lifetime of history. No one, other than my mom and dad, has known me longer, loved me longer. I will never again forget the value of this. Despite the way we've been tested, I love her and always will.

Chapter Forty-nine

"There is a saying in Tibetan, 'Tragedy should be utilized as a source of strength.' No matter what sort of difficulties, how painful experience is, if we lose our hope, that's our real disaster."
— Dalai Lama

Catherine

I'M IN THE cafeteria on the main floor of the hospital getting a salad I am admittedly tired of as the mainstay of my diet when I hear someone say my name.

The voice sends a wave of shock rippling through me. I go still, sure I've imagined it.

Slowly, I turn around. "Anders."

He looks uncertain, as if he isn't sure I will be happy to see him. "Hi," he says.

"Hi," I say back, my gaze taking in the unbelievably wonderful sight of him. He's dressed in faded jeans and a white button-down shirt, his tan skin visible at his throat and arms where the sleeves are rolled up. My heart is beating so fast I can feel it against my chest. "What—"

"I should have called. But I knew you would tell me not to come."

I start to deny it. He's right though. I would have. I'm suddenly remembering what I must look like, all remnants of my own sun-kissed skin gone beneath the hospital's fluorescent light pallor. My hair is pulled back in a ponytail, and I haven't bothered to put on makeup since I got here. "I look—"

"Beautiful," he says.

"Hah. No."

"I was headed to the information desk when I saw you in here."

"I can't believe you came."

"I wanted to see you. Make sure you're okay."

The words are sincere, and the look in his eyes tells me he means it. "I don't know what to say." I shake my head, overcome with emotion.

"Just say it's okay I'm here."

"It is. I—"

"Look like you could use a hug."

The tears well up then, and I have no ability to stop them. He reaches for me, pulls me into the circle of his arms and locks me there. I tuck my face to his chest, sobs shaking my shoulders. He presses a kiss to the top of my head, and I melt beneath the need to be comforted by a man I cannot deny caring about.

In a few moments, he takes my hand and leads me from the cafeteria. We walk outside and into the small park to one side of the hospital. He leads me to an enormous tree lending shade to the grassy area.

He leans against the wide trunk and pulls me to him again. He feels as strong as this tree, able to weather the darkest of storms, and I'm not ashamed to admit now I need his strength. I slip my arms around his neck and press myself to him. I cry against his chest, sobs pouring out from somewhere deep inside me, shaking my shoulders and leaving me weak beneath the release.

And he just holds me, rubbing the back of my hair with one hand, saying nothing, as if he knows there aren't any words that will dissolve the pain. There is only comfort for acknowledgement of this, and it is only in receiving it that I realize how much I need it.

I don't know how long we stand there, anchored against that tree trunk with a soft breeze whispering against us. But at some point, my tears stop, and I am now quiet against him, weak with release.

He puts his hands on my shoulders and pushes me back far enough to look into my face. "I've missed you."

"I've missed you."

"There are plenty of reasons we don't make sense. I get that. They don't matter though. Because I know how you make me feel. I love where I live and the life I've made there. But since you left . . . it's not the same."

I absorb this admission, and wonder if I've imagined what he's just said. This man. . .this beautiful man wants me. And I want him. All the reasons I presented to myself as to why we wouldn't work won't materialize in my brain. I grapple for them, but they no longer form into anything I can make sense of. "Are you sure?"

"I've never been more sure of anything."

I put my hands to either side of his face, lean up and kiss him. Softly at first, and then deeper, gasping when he swoops me up and takes the lead, kissing me with physical proof of his confession. And I have no desire to hide what I feel for him. What is the point? Life is here. Right in front of us. We can reach for it and find the happiness being together provides us. Or let it slip away to be nothing but a memory of what could have been.

I reach for it with no intention of ever letting it go. And he feels the change in me. Because he slips an arm to the back of my legs and swoops me up, carrying me to a nearby bench and sitting down with me on his lap. We kiss until we both begin to believe we really are together, and that we'll find our way forward to a place where a life with each other is not only possible, but definite.

"I love you," he says, leaning back to stare into my eyes so I can see that love like my own reflection in a perfectly still lake. "What I've been thinking is that just because I recognized it nearly from the moment I met you, does that make it a lesser love? It doesn't," he adds, answering his own question.

My heart is full, so full that I have nothing but truth for him. "I love you. I do."

He kisses me softly.

And then I say, "It won't be easy."

"No. But it will be worth it."

"Yes. It will."

We sit for a while, peaceful in the knowledge that whatever lies ahead, we'll be facing it together. And when we're ready, I stand, take his hand and lead him inside the hospital to meet the rest of my family.

Epilogue

"There are only two ways to live your life. One is as though nothing is a miracle. The other is as though everything is a miracle."

— Albert Einstein

Anders

IT'S ONE OF those days that could be used for a postcard shot of Needham's Point Beach. The sun has dipped its lowest against the horizon, pink tendrils of light lacing the still blue sky. There's a crowd on the beach this evening. Over one hundred babies to release tonight, according to Hannah. The most they've had in a good while.

"Da-da!"

I turn to see Evie toddling toward me in the sand, her arms outstretched. Her blonde hair hangs in braids, a pink ribbon at the end of each. I swoop her up, parking her on my hip and brushing sand from her sun-brown little feet.

"Evie turtle?" she asks.

"I'm sure Hannah will have a turtle for you to help."

A smile breaks across her delighted face, and my heart is crushed yet again with love for her.

"Hey."

Catherine touches my shoulder, leans up to kiss my cheek. "Sorry we're late. I had one last phone call to make, and Evie took a long nap this afternoon."

"You're just in time," I say, leaning in to kiss her on the lips, taking my time with it.

Footsteps sound behind us, and I look up. Nicole walks across the sand, her dog Callie trotting along beside her. Ever since Nicole adopted her from the shelter she volunteers at in West Palm Beach, the dog does her best to never leave her side, traveling with her on visits here as an emotional support companion. Like Nicole, she's become a seasoned traveler to Barbados. "Hey," I say, glancing around Nicole and adding, "Luke came, didn't he?"

She smiles her quiet smile and says, "He's back there talking to Hannah. He's fascinated with the turtles and wants to know everything he can learn about them."

"He's in good company then," I say.

Nicole reaches out to brush a few more grains of sand from Evie's leg, and I take the moment to wonder at the difference in her. I think of the pale gray woman I met in the hospital in West Palm Beach three years ago and this rejuvenated version beside me now. She has fought her way back from a depression that robbed her of all will to live to the place where she is now, aware that she will have to take care of herself in the ways people with depression have to in order to stay well. She's coming to the island to visit us every three months or so, and this time she brought Luke with her, a guy she met at the animal shelter. He founded the sanctuary with part of an inheritance from his grandmother, and it seems as if the two of them have found something in each other that fits. Not unlike Catherine and me. Their puzzle is different from ours, but the pieces go together just the same.

I drape my arm around Catherine's shoulder and tuck her against me as we take in the sun setting before us. Hannah and a few of her volunteers start across the beach with the trays of tiny turtles.

"Evie see! Evie see!"

"Hold on now," I say, laughing and setting Evie on the sand in front of me.

"We have to be gentle with them, sweetie," Catherine says, smiling. "I remember the first time I saw this," she says, squatting down to look our daughter in the eyes. "I was so excited I could barely contain myself."

"Where turtles go, Mama?" Evie asks.

Catherine hesitates and then, "Home, baby. They're going home."

Hannah approaches with one of the trays, drops to her knees next to us and reaches for Evie's hand. Evie looks down at the baby turtles, her eyes wide with awe.

"Pick one up, sweetie," Catherine says. "Just be very, very gentle."

Evie reaches down and takes one with a kindness

that makes my heart swell. "Okay," I say, picking one up and showing her how to set it in the firmer sand.

She sets hers next to mine and smiles a smile of delight as they take off for the ocean. "Turtle go home," she says, and there's now sadness in her voice.

I put my hand on her head and rub her hair. "It's okay, honey. Home is where they want to be. It's where they'll be happy."

She raises her arms for me to pick her up. I do, and we watch as the rest of the baby turtles are released and head for the water. "When they grow up, they might come back to visit one day," I say.

I put an arm around Catherine, and the three of us stay there until all the babies have found their way to the sea. Catherine looks up at me, and I see in her eyes what I am thinking. Life is hard. But life is beautiful. And it will always, always be worth the struggle.

***

The Barbados Sea Turtle Project

I really can't find the words to describe how much I am moved by the beautiful sea turtles who struggle against great odds to survive and thrive in the ocean that is their home. Below are some pics of our family trip to Barbados where we got to see them for the first time.

If you would like to learn more about them, please visit Barbados Sea Turtles. You can also Like their Facebook page and receive updates about releases and other fascinating information about the ongoing effort to preserve these magnificent creatures. You can make a donation to help the Barbados Sea Turtle Project here.

Inglath Cooper

Book Club Guide

1. What made you decide to read *That Birthday in Barbados*?
2. How did you feel about the characters?
3. Why do you think Catherine was blind to the affair between Connor and Nicole?
4. Do you think it is possible for siblings to deeply love each other but also have very complicated layers to the relationship? How so and why?
5. Escape is a central theme in the book. Do you believe people sometimes need to remove themselves from their regular lives to see other ways of living?
6. What do you think of the older woman, younger man dynamic? Do you think age differences matter?
7. What did Anders' illness lead him to realize about life? Was he willing to die

rather than live in a way that did not make sense to him?

8. Forgiveness is a central theme in the book. Do you think it is possible to forgive a loved one for unimaginable betrayal? Should Catherine have forgiven Nicole sooner than she did?
9. Why did Catherine and Nicole keep the truth about their fractured relationship from their parents?
10. Nicole experiences the callousness of people who leave devoted pets at shelters. How do you think realizing what happens to many of them affected her? Do you think most people know what happens in these types of shelters? Do you think if they did, they would want it to change?
11. The quote from David Foster Wallace – You'd have to have personally been trapped and felt flames to really understand a terror way beyond falling. – What do you think he is saying about people who choose to take their own lives? Do you think Nicole could see no other way to right her wrong? Or that her own depression was beyond enduring?
12. Catherine realizes that life is a continuous blend of good and bad, hard and easy, miraculous and horrifying. How do we accept this constant state of contradiction

about life, and what makes it all bearable?

13. What do you think Catherine and Anders find in each other?
14. What do the sea turtles represent for you in the story? Do you see a comparison between their incredible will to live and the struggle they face to survive and Anders' own will to live?
15. What is your favorite scene in the book?
16. How do you picture the lives of the characters after the story is over?
17. Did this book make you think about anything in your own life differently?
18. Would you recommend *That Birthday in Barbados* to a reader friend? If so, why?

If You Enjoyed That Birthday in Barbados. . .

that
month
in tuscany
I never thought I'd see Italy with a rock star! But I felt like I did when I read this book! - Amazon.com Reviewer
Award Winning Author
INGLATH COOPER

Excerpt from That Month in Tuscany

Lizzy

IF I'M HONEST with myself, truly honest, I will admit I knew that in the end, he wouldn't go.

But to leave it until the night before: that surprises even me.

Here I sit on my over-packed suitcase in the foyer of this too large house I've spent the past five years decorating and fussing over — picking out paint colors and rugs, which include the exact same shade, and art that can only be hung on the walls if it looks like an original, even if it isn't.

I stare at the pair of tickets in my hand, open the folder and read the schedule as I have a dozen times before.

Departure Charlotte, North Carolina 3:45 PM
Arrival Rome, Italy 7:30 AM
Departure Rome, Italy 9:40 AM
Arrival Florence, Italy 10:45 AM

My name on one: Millicent Elizabeth Harper. His on the other: Tyler Fraiser Harper.

I bought the tickets six months ago. Plenty of time to plan how to get away from the office for a month. Make whatever arrangements had to be made. Didn't people do things like that now and then? Check out of their real lives for a bit? Let others take over in their absence?

Tyler's response would be, "Yeah, people who don't care about their careers. People who don't mind risking everything they've worked for by letting some Ivy League know-it-all step into their shoes long enough to prove that they can fill them."

Our twentieth anniversary is tomorrow. I'd imagined that we would arrive at the Hotel Savoy and celebrate with a bottle of Italian champagne in a room where we could spend the next month getting to know one another again — the way we had once known one another. Traveling around the Tuscan countryside on day trips and eating lunch in small town trattorias. Exploring art museums and local artisan shops.

I shared all of this with him, and he had done a fine job of making me believe that he found it as appealing as I did. It felt as if we again had a common interest after years of a life divided into his and hers, yours and mine.

Then, a little over a week ago, he'd begun to plant the seeds of backpedaling. I had just finished putting together a salad for our dinner when my cell phone rang.

It lay buzzing on the kitchen counter, and

something in my stomach, even at that moment, told me that he would back out.

I started not to answer, as if that would change the course of the demolition he was about to execute on the trip I had been dreaming of our entire married life. Actually, maybe the trip was a metaphor for what I had hoped would be the resurrection of our marriage during a month away together. The two of us, Ty and me like it used to be when we first started dating, and it didn't matter what we were doing as long as we did it together.

Ironically, we've had the house to ourselves for almost two years now. It's hard to believe that Kylie's been away at college for that long, but she has. Almost two years during which I've continued to wait for Ty's promises of less time at the office and more time at home to actually bear fruit; only they never have.

And I guess this is what it has taken to make me see that they never will.

Me, sitting on a suitcase, alone in our house, waiting for something that's not going to happen. Waiting for Ty to realize that we hardly even know each other anymore; waiting for him to remember how much he had once loved me; waiting for him to miss me.

I feel my phone vibrate in the pocket of my jacket. I know without looking that it's Ty. Calling to make sure I've canceled our tickets and gotten as much of a refund as I can, considering that it's last minute. I know that he'll also want to make sure I'm back to my cheerful self. He'll be waiting for the note of impending forgiveness in my voice, the one that tells him he doesn't need to feel guilty. I'll be here, as I always have. Things happen. Plans get changed. Buck up, and move on.

I pull the phone from my pocket, stare at his name on the screen.

I lift my thumb to tap Answer. I'm poised to do every one of the things that Ty expects of me. I really am. Then I picture myself alone in this house every day from six-thirty to eight o'clock at night. And I just can't stand the thought of it.

I actually feel physically ill. I realize in that moment that I am at a crossroad. Stay and lose myself forever to someone I had never imagined I would be. Go and maybe, maybe, start to resurrect the real me. Or find out if she is actually gone forever.

The moment hangs. My stomach drops under the weight of my decision. I hit End Call and put the phone back in my pocket. And without looking back, I pick up my suitcase and walk out the door.

~

I PARK IN THE long-term lot and not in the back, either, where Ty would insist that I leave the BMW. I park it smack dab up front, tight in between a well-dented mini-van and a Ford Taurus with peeling paint. It is the very last parking space Ty would pick and petty as it sounds, I get enormous pleasure from the fact that my door has to touch the other vehicle in order for me to squeeze out.

I get my suitcase out of the trunk, letting it drop to the pavement with a hard thunk. I roll it to the white airport shuttle waiting at the curb. An older man with a kind face gets out and takes my bag from me, lifting it up the stairs with enough effort that I wish he'd let me do it myself.

Then he smiles at me, and I realize he doesn't mind.

There are two people already on the shuttle, sitting in the back. They are absorbed in each other, the woman laughing at something the man has said. I deliberately don't look at them, keeping my gaze focused over the shoulder of the driver who is now whistling softly.

"What gate, ma'am?" he asks, looking up at me in the rearview mirror.

"United," I answer.

"You got it," he says, and goes back to his whistling.

I feel my phone vibrating in the pocket of my black coat. I try to resist the urge to look at who's calling, but my hand reaches for it automatically.

Ty. It's the third time he's called since I left the house. I put the phone back in my pocket.

When we arrive at the United gate, the whistling driver again helps me with my suitcase. I drop a tip in the cup by the door and thank him.

"You're most welcome, dear. Where you headed?"

"Italy," I say.

He lifts his eyebrows and says, "I always wanted to see that place. You going by yourself?"

"Yes," I answer. It's only then that I'm absolutely sure I am really doing this.

I am doing this.

~

THE CHECK-IN process is lengthy. When the woman behind the desk asks me about my husband's ticket, I tell her that he will be along shortly. Lying isn't something I'm in the habit of doing, but I don't think I can admit to her that he isn't coming without unraveling an explanation that might keep us both here way past the plane's departure time.

"Hopefully, he'll be here soon," she says. "Don't want to cut it too close. These international flights leave promptly."

I simply nod. She asks to see my passport, compares the picture with my face, and types a whole bunch of things into the computer. What, I cannot imagine because they already have all my information. A full five minutes tick by before she hands me the boarding pass.

Taking it from her feels like the closing of a door that I will not be able to reopen. As metaphors go, I have to think it's pretty accurate.

The security process is almost reason enough for me to stop flying altogether. If I could get to Italy by car, I would most certainly drive.

The underwire in my bra instigates a pat-down by a woman who looks as if she's no happier about the procedure than I am. She asks me in a cigarette-roughened voice if I would rather have this conducted in a private room. Since I suppose that means she and I would be the only two occupants, I choose public embarrassment instead.

Once my bra passes the feel-up check, I am directed through the booth where I have to spread my legs and raise my arms in the same posture criminals are told to take by their arresting officer. Not for the first time, I resent the heck out of the bad people who caused all of us trying-hard-to-be-good ones to have to go through this.

An oversize purse is my only carry-on and once my laptop and camera come through the conveyor belt, I stick them back inside.

I head for the concourse that my plane will be leaving from. Boarding begins in less than an hour, so I buy a few snacks and use the ladies room. I find a seat in the chairs by the gate. It looks as if the flight will be full, based on the number of people already here. The thought of an overbooked, way-too-full flight makes my stomach drop.

I cannot remember the last time I went anywhere by myself. I'm used to Ty carrying the tickets, checking in the luggage while Kylie and I hover in the background, handing over our identification when prompted, and checking email on our phones.

I pull out my phone now and glance at the screen, noticing a text message. I click in and see that it's from Winn.

Lizzy!!! U and Ty have the time of your lives. I CANNOT wait to hear all about it. I just know u 2 are going to come back like newlyweds. Shoot, Ty might even leave the firm, and y'all can travel around indefinitely the way u always dreamed about.

The message blurs before my eyes, the tears there before I can even think to will them away. I tap in a response.

Ty's not going.

I hit send, and it seems as if the reply is nearly instantaneous.

What?!!?

The phone vibrates. Winn's name pops up on the screen. I hit answer and put it to my ear. "Yes, I know. I was a fool to think he really would."

"Lizzy." My name is drawn out into at least six syllables. I hear her devastation. It's nearly as thick and heartbroken as my own. "What? Why?"

"A new case," I say.

"Are you kidding me?" she asks, the question lit with instant fury. While there's really nothing to be gained from it, it kind of feels nice to have someone see things from my point of view.

"I can't believe he would do this to you. It's your twentieth anniversary."

"Yes," I say. "It is."

"He doesn't deserve you, Lizzy. He never did."

"You're just saying that because you're mad. No one wanted us to be together more than you."

"Well, I was wrong. I'm a big enough person to admit that."

I almost smile at this. Ty has never had a bigger fan than Winn. In fact, I think she's been a little secretly in love with him since the day we both met him in English Lit at UVa.

"And what do you mean," she asks suddenly, "Ty's not going? Are *you* going?"

I glance around at the other passengers, and the whole thing feels surreal, like a dream I'm going to wake up from at any moment. "Yes," I say, again making my decision reality.

At least three seconds of silence tick by before she says, "Wow."

"You think I'm crazy."

"I think you're right. It's exactly what you should do. But I can't believe you're actually going to."

"There's something in there that should make me feel less than good."

"You know what I mean. How many times has he done this to you? That trip to the Caribbean after our ten-year reunion. The ski trip last winter—"

"I know," I say, stopping her. "I don't need to hear the list of times Ty has disappointed me. Because if I do, I'm also going to remember that I've pretty much been a doormat for him to wipe his feet on."

"I wish I could go with you," Winn says. "Are you staying the whole month?"

"That's my plan."

And then as if she remembers the reason I'm going alone, she says, "I'm really sorry, Lizzy. You don't deserve this. You deserve so much better."

"Spilled milk and all that," I say.

"It's his loss. One day, he's going to realize that. What did he say when you said you were going without him?"

"Um, he doesn't know yet."

Again, silence, processing, and then, "Are you sure this is Lizzy Harper?"

I actually laugh at this.

"I am incredulous. It's what you should have done a long time ago, you know," she says softly.

"Probably no denying that."

"He needs a good wake-up call."

"You know, Winn, it's not even about that. I'm doing this for me."

"Good. Good," she repeats. "How do I get in touch with you?"

"Once I leave the states, my phone will be useless. I didn't sign up for the international plan because I thought it would be nice for the two of us to cut off all communications from home for the time we were there. Ironic, isn't it?"

"But how will I know how you're doing?"

"I'll check in by email, if I have wireless."

"You promise?"

"I promise."

"I love you, Lizzy. I'm proud of you."

"You're just saying that because I'm so pathetic."

"Pathetic would be you canceling the trip."

"Yeah?"

"Yeah."

"And don't spend all of your time walking through museums and old churches and stuff. Find something fun to do. *Someone* fun to—"

"Winn!"

She laughs. "It would serve him right."

"You know that's not me."

"Maybe it should be you."

"Like that would fix my life."

"Might not fix your life, but it would definitely fix the moment."

I smile and shake my head. "You'd make a terrible shrink."

"But an excellent friend."

"I'll give you that."

"Roanoke won't be the same without you."

"It's only a month."

"Let me hear from you."

"I will," I say, adding, "Be good."

"Only if you promise not to be."

Books by Inglath Cooper

That Birthday in Barbados
That Month in Tuscany
Swerve
The Heart That Breaks
My Italian Lover
Fences – Book Three – Smith Mountain Lake Series
Dragonfly Summer – Book Two – Smith Mountain Lake Series
Blue Wide Sky – Book One – Smith Mountain Lake Series
And Then You Loved Me
Down a Country Road
Good Guys Love Dogs
Truths and Roses
Nashville – Part Ten – Not Without You
Nashville – Book Nine – You, Me and a Palm Tree
Nashville – Book Eight – R U Serious
Nashville – Book Seven – Commit
Nashville – Book Six – Sweet Tea and Me

Nashville – Book Five – Amazed
Nashville – Book Four – Pleasure in the Rain
Nashville – Book Three – What We Feel
Nashville – Book Two – Hammer and a Song
Nashville – Book One – Ready to Reach
A Gift of Grace
RITA® Award Winner John Riley's Girl
A Woman With Secrets
Unfinished Business
A Woman Like Annie
The Lost Daughter of Pigeon Hollow
A Year and a Day

Dear Reader

I would like to thank you for taking the time to read my story. There are so many wonderful books to choose from these days, and I am hugely appreciative that you chose mine.

Please join my mailing list for updates on new releases and giveaways! Just go to http://www.inglathcooper.com – come check out my Facebook page for postings on books, dogs and things that make life good!

Wishing you many, many happy afternoons of reading pleasure.

All best,

Inglath

About Inglath Cooper

RITA® Award-winning author Inglath Cooper was born in Virginia. She is a graduate of Virginia Tech with a degree in English. She fell in love with books as soon as she learned how to read. "My mom read to us before bed, and I think that's how I started to love stories. It was like a little mini-vacation we looked forward to every night before going to sleep. I think I eventually read most of the books in my elementary school library."

That love for books translated into a natural love for writing and a desire to create stories that other readers could get lost in, just as she had gotten lost in her favorite books. Her stories focus on the dynamics of relationships, those between a man and a woman, mother and daughter, sisters, friends.

Inglath Cooper is an avid supporter of companion animal rescue and is a volunteer and donor for the Franklin County Humane Society. She and her family have fostered many dogs and cats that have gone on to be adopted by other families. "The rewards are endless. It's an eye-opening moment to realize that what one person throws away can fill another person's life with love and joy."

Follow Inglath on Facebook at www.facebook.com/inglathcooperbooks

Join her mailing list for news of new releases and giveaways at www.inglathcooper.com